I'm not brave enough, she thought.

But now it was seven o'clock on Saturday night, and the dance began at eight, and now she had to carry the plan out. She, the C girl, the average girl, had to put the dress on, and actually appear at that dance.

Alone.

Panic washed over her like a rising tide, carrying with it the debris of all her past failures. I won't be able to carry it off, she thought. I'll be laughed at. I'll stumble around the walls of the cafeteria and end up with some teacher trying to be nice. I'll sit on some metal folding chair for two hours while the teacher tries to think of something to say.

She drew the plastic bag off the dress. The bag clung to the dress, as if not wanting to leave the shimmery pink and the gray lace and she thought, *Please let me look lovely in it.* Please let it work this time, too. Let me be special!

Saturday Night

Caroline B. Cooney

SCHOLASTIC INC.
New York Toronto London Auckland Sydney

Cover: Dress by FLIRTATION, a division of Alfred Angelo.

ISBN 0-590-40156-4

Copyright © 1986 by Caroline B. Cooney. All rights reserved. Published by Scholastic Inc.

12 11 10 9 8 7 6 5 4 3 2 1   8   6 7 8 9/8 0 1/9

Printed in the U.S.A.   01

Saturday Night

Prologue

Five girls sat before their mirrors, playing with eye shadow, blusher, electric curlers, and jewelry. Saturday night, and a formal dance. Lovely gowns, sparkling necklaces, throbbing music, sweetly scented flowers.

But the five girls were thinking only of love. And one girl was loved too much, and one was not loved at all.

Thunder rolled across the autumn sky like an announcement that it was time to leave for the dance. Lightning streaked above the bare branches of the trees, and the last leaves whirled through the blackness of night and settled on the wet pavement.

Tonight, both the loveliest of dreams and the worst of nightmares would come true.

Chapter 1

Beth Rose Chapman went to the dance because of a dress.

Not *a* dress, really. *The* dress.

Beth Rose had no fashion sense. No matter what she put on, when she got to school, it turned out to be wrong. She had a remarkable ability, she thought sadly, to look dowdy. I'm sixteen, thought Beth Rose, and I'm already matronly.

If she chose bright colors, they clashed. If she chose pastels, she looked like a hospital patient. Gathered skirts made her look plump and tight skirts rode up her knees and bunched at the thigh.

But not this dress.

It was her great aunt's. A month ago Beth was visiting her Aunt Madge and found it wrapped in a clear plastic dry cleaner's bag, hanging on a rack in the attic. "I wore that to my senior prom in 1938," said Aunt Madge, smiling gently to herself, touching the bag, but not the dress within.

Beth Rose stared at the dress. A very soft gleaming pink. She was not permitted to wear pink. She had dark red hair and her mother categorically stated that pink was impossible. Aunt Madge and Beth Rose stood silently, admiring the dress. Aunt Madge said, "Try it on, Bethie."

She tried it on.

Such an old-fashioned dress, and yet not one where people would giggle at her; not a dress where people would wonder why it hadn't been given to the Salvation Army decades ago. Its style was unusual, but timeless. There were three fabrics: one of glistening pink and one of delicate, faintly gray lace (but Aunt Madge said it had always been gray). Then there were tiny bows of silvery ribbon tipped with pink along the sleeves, dancing from the falling shoulders to the tight lace-cuffed wrists.

Aunt Madge had an enormous old mirror set in a mahogany frame that tilted back and forth. They tipped the mirror until Beth Rose was captured from her hair to her bare toes. "But my hair is red," said Beth.

"The pink is so pale it doesn't matter," said her Aunt Madge. "Anyhow, your hair is the loveliest red I know. Dark, not gaudy. Gleaming, not bristly."

Beth Rose touched her hair. Her mother always groaned whenever they went to the hairdresser. The hairdresser always groaned. Her hair was thick and unmanageable and uncooperative. It didn't matter what shampoos and conditioners they used, it never changed. Beth thought it looked like a wig for someone who had had brain surgery.

"Needs braiding," said Aunt Madge, and her fingers began twisting and plaiting in Beth's hair until the top had become a flattened cap of narrow braids that rested on thick waves falling to her bare shoulders.

The neckline of the old prom dress dipped in scallops edged with the old gray lace. "I look so fragile," breathed Beth, "as if I'm a museum piece."

"What you look," said Aunt Madge briskly, "is perfect. No question about it, Brose. You must find an important dance and wear this dress."

Beth Rose stared into the mirror for a long time. The dress was a Cinderella dress. Transforming. In it she felt herself to be everything the dress was: soft, gleaming, fragile, timelessly lovely. "But I'm not really like that," she said sadly. "In school I'm so ordinary, Aunt Madge. I'm always a C."

"What's a C?" said Aunt Madge.

"Average. I get a C in English and I get a C in math. I get a C in gym and all my friends are C-type people. A-plus people don't even know I'm alive. And this — this is an A-plus dress."

"Which needs an A-plus occasion," said her aunt.

The girl touched her hair, her cheeks, her throat. She could not believe that lovely reflection was her. She said slowly, "Well, there's the Autumn Leaves Dance. First week in November."

"That's that, then," said Aunt Madge. She gently took the dress from Beth's shoulders, undoing the long, long row of tiny fabric-covered buttons in back, and put it up on its padded hanger.

"Why Bethie," Aunt Madge exclaimed, when she had finished slipping the dry cleaner's bag over the dress again, "you're crying! Sweetheart, what's the matter?"

She could weep with her aunt. She never dared weep in front of her mother. Her mother just got impatient. "If you'd only try harder," her mother would snap, as if Beth hadn't struggled all her life with all her energy. But Aunt Madge never did that. Aunt Madge said, "Tell me, darling, is it the dress? What is it?"

"It's me. I can't go to the Autumn Leaves Dance because nobody will ask me. I'm not the kind of girl boys ask."

Her mother would have said, "Nonsense." Or else, "If you'd just try to be more attractive, easier to get along with. . . ."

Aunt Madge made comforting little noises and rocked Beth as if she were an infant. She said, "Can you go alone to this dance or is it for couples only?"

"Well, you *could* go alone," said Beth. "Some boys will. But girls? They just don't. I couldn't do that."

"In this dress you could do anything," Aunt Madge said.

Through the flimsy bag the dress had an ethereal look to it, like a pink cloud of summer sunset blown by the wind. Beth Rose said, "I'm not brave enough, Aunt Madge."

Her mother would have said, "Nonsense, Beth. Don't be a 'fraidy cat."

Aunt Madge said, "Nobody's that brave. To go alone and know you'll stand alone all evening while everybody else is a couple? Especially if there's a lot of hand-holding and kissing. That's the worst part. You stand there in some dreary corner, trying to look as if you *like* being alone. And of course everybody knows you're a fake, and they stay away from you so they won't catch whatever disease you're carrying." Aunt Madge shuddered.

"So you see I can't go," said Beth Rose.

"Yes, you can. The dress will make you different."

It was true. The dress had changed her. "Just think of me as your fairy godmother," Aunt Madge said softly, and she waved a graceful wrist, its blue veins showing as if she were holding a magic wand. "And now you're going to the ball to meet the handsome prince."

And of course Beth couldn't resist. She took the dress home to Westerly and hung it in her closet and touched it like a magic charm every morning and evening, and bought herself a ticket to Autumn Leaves.

But now it was seven o'clock on Saturday night, and the dance began at eight, and now she had to carry the plan out. She, the C girl, the average girl, had to put the dress on and actually appear at that dance.

Alone.

Panic washed over Beth like a rising tide, carrying with it the debris of all her past failures. I won't be able to carry it off, thought Beth Rose. I'll be laughed at. I'll stumble around the walls of the cafeteria and end up with some teacher trying to be nice. I'll sit on some metal folding chair for two hours while the teacher tries to think of something to say.

She drew the plastic bag off the dress. The bag clung to the dress, as if not wanting to leave the shimmery pink and the gray lace, and Beth Rose thought, *Please let me look lovely in it.* Please let it work this time, too. Let me be special!

Chapter 2

Anne Stephens was the A-plus Beth was thinking of when she said no one ever noticed her. Beth was right. Anne had never even known Beth existed until this year, when they were in the same gym class and played volleyball on the same side of the net. Anne always served perfectly. Beth Rose always missed and afterwards her wrist hurt.

Anne found her mildly irritating. A person should be able to do *something* right.

But Beth Rose Chapman's lack of ability was the last thing on Anne's mind at seven o'clock the night of the Autumn Leaves Dance.

Anne, too, had a full length mirror, but when she stood before it she saw nothing but perfection. Anne was unarguably the loveliest girl in the junior class at Westerly High. However, she was a little tired of seeing *three* reflections in her mirror every time she got ready to go out with Con.

Her mother and grandmother participated in her dates as much as she did, Anne sometimes thought. They loved Anne's perfection, they loved dressing her — as if she were a very tall Barbie doll — and they loved the sight and the thought of Anne with Con.

Her grandmother had bought her tonight's dress. The older women took turns outfitting Anne. She was probably the only girl in the state whose family was dying to buy more clothes for her at any time.

The dress for this, her first formal dance, was layers of deep electric blue, jaggedly cut, so that the skirt swirled unexpectedly, shifting with every breath, making soft whispery sounds as the brilliant blue fabric slid over itself. The neckline was not symmetrical, and her grandmother had had Anne's hair done so that it was swept to the side, and offset the unusual neckline, and then bought Anne a rhinestone necklace with an art-deco star that trembled just below her throat, and another one to go in her hair. The sleeves were beaded, tiny tiny beads of exactly the same color as the dress, so that in some lights you couldn't tell the beads were there, and in other lights Anne sent rainbows across the room as if she were hung with prisms.

Anne ran her fingertips over the beaded patterns. How strange they felt beneath her fingers! How smooth, and absolutely perfect.

Her mother adjusted the thick sash, moving it a little too high so that Anne twitched with wanting to push it back down. Her grandmother took out the rhinestone star in her hair and moved it an inch farther back, so that Anne could no longer see it, just feel its unaccustomed weight. Her hair was thick and gold, in as many layers as her dress, and its waves swept up majestically on one side and lay flat on the other.

"She's perfect," said Anne's mother contentedly.

This was the final sentence Mrs. Stephens uttered before all of Anne's dates. Anne smiled, fulfilling her part of the tradition, but she did not meet her mother's eyes, even in the mirror. Because she was not perfect; in the last few weeks she had found out just how imperfect she really was; and if her mother knew. . . .

"You know what?" Anne's grandmother said. "This must be just about your third anniversary, too."

Yes, Anne thought. We were in junior high. Con was scrawny, with a shape rather like a chewed-on pencil. His hair was still being cut at home, and his mother was so bad at it he looked as if he had fur instead of hair. But I liked him. Oh, how I liked him!

In ninth grade, Con grew seven inches. You could practically sit at the table and watch him grow. He was awkward that year, and never got off the bench in any of his beloved sports, because he could not control those suddenly long limbs. And then the following summer, his complexion cleared, his hair filled in, his braces came off, and his coordination returned.

And he was handsome, and dark, and suave, and he knew it. Oh, how he knew it! Con would never admit it, but he was as fond of perfection as Anne's mother. They weren't seniors, but she knew that their yearbook the following year would have herself and Con as Couple of the Class. She was idolized by the younger girls. She, Anne Stephens, had the life and the boy they all yearned for, daydreamed for, maybe even prayed for.

Anne bit down on her lower lip, feeling suddenly as if she might throw up. Instantly her mother and grandmother were next to her, anxious, wanting to be convinced that all was well. "I'm fine," said Anne. "Just nervous."

"Nervous? You?" They both laughed.

I have to get away from them, she thought. Just for a minute to pull myself together. But in the Stephens household there was no privacy. Never had been. Anne was community property here, even at seventeen years of age. "I have to go to the bathroom," she told them, and shut the door on their warnings not to muss her dress.

Nothing to be nervous about, Anne thought, and she wanted to laugh, but she didn't dare. She had a feeling that if she laughed even a little bit, the laugh would grow into hysteria and she would turn insane on the spot.

Oh, Con, she thought, what are you going to say?

She didn't really care what he would say, though. Con was not much of a talker. Even after three years of constant dating, Anne sometimes had the sensation that she didn't know Con. He had a way of allocating his personality: he would permit a specific fraction to show at any given time, and the rest he kept to himself.

It was not what he would say that worried her.

It was what he would do.

Tonight is truth time, Anne thought, staring into the smaller, much more brightly lit bathroom mirror. I think of Con as my rock, my life. But I don't know that. We're at the crunch, we're at the top of the cliff, and I don't know if I trust him. How strange. How awful. To love him as much as I do, and not trust him.

She tried to kill the thought, as if it could filter out of the bathroom, travel across town, curl around Con's mind, and whisper to him, *She doesn't trust you.*

Anne was shivering. She couldn't see the shivers in the mirror. She felt them on the inside, and her flesh crawled and turned cold.

Tonight. She would have to talk with him tonight.

For the first time in three years, Anne was sorry that she and Con had gotten so close. Because she had no intimate girl friend to talk to. She had let them all drift away, sure that Con could be everything and everyone to her. And now when she needed advice, there was not a telephone number in all Westerly she could really dial and find a friend.

I'm the most popular girl in Westerly, she thought, numbed with fear, and I'm the most alone. How did *that* happen? How *could* that happen? If you're popular, then by definition you can't be all alone.

I'm all alone.

I don't even know if Con is here.

Through the door her mother said, "Darling, you're not changing your makeup, are you? I really think it was perfect."

Perfect. A person could come to hate that word after a few years, Anne thought. "No, Mother," she said.

For all that Mrs. Stephens had had a grim, poor childhood, she was really very innocent. For her there had been no happy adolescence: no dances, no dates, no boys in gleaming cars. Only Anne's father — who was abroad more than half the year, selling blue jeans in Europe — had rescued her from that grinding poverty. And the greatest joy in Mrs. Stephen's life was Anne; and Anne's looks, and talent, and brains, and boyfriend.

In school, Anne and Con were taking a gut course called Family Relations. The only reason anybody took this was to get three easy credits, and be able to talk quietly during filmstrips. But surprisingly, Family Relations was quite interesting. In the third week of class Con said to her, "That's your mother. Right here listed under Classic Examples. It's the old Smother Mother routine."

"She doesn't smother me," objected Anne.

"She sure tries hard enough," Con said, whose goal with the Stephens family was to get in and out the door with Anne as quickly as possible, and not have to hear what a perfect couple they made.

"I love her, though," said Anne mildly.

"Yeah, but you have low standards," Con told her.

Anne laughed. "Low?" she repeated. "To love a mother like mine? To love my grandmother, too, even though they both interfere around the clock? You should try it some time, Connie. It takes one heck of a lot of effort to keep up those low standards of mine."

Standards, Anne thought, opening the bathroom door. What kind of standards do I have? I don't know anymore.

"Oh, Anne," breathed her mother yet again, "oh, sweetheart, you look so lovely."

Con would not say it. He never noticed how she looked. It was one of their problems. Anne was accustomed to her own personal cheering section. Even when they infuriated her, her two fans at home could be counted on to list her various beauties and talents. Not Con. He'd just say, "What'll we do Friday? I'm sick of going to the movies."

She'd told him and told him that her dress for the Autumn Leaves Dance was electric blue and she wanted white flowers. Heavily scented. But if she knew Con (and she did) he wouldn't remember flowers at all. But if she knew her mother (and she did) Mrs. Stephens would have phoned in the flowers in Con's name, and called Con to let him know, and Con would show up with the right flowers and everybody would pretend Con had done it.

Once Con had said, "You'd better not turn out to be like your mother. Tough and domineering."

Anne thought, I'd be better off if I were tough and domineering. I've given in to everyone all my life, and I never even knew it till now. I never even noticed. I was so busy being perfectly beautiful and popular and smart I didn't notice that I've never made a single decision in my life. Not stupid ones, not good ones. Con's just as domineering as they are. And I never knew that, either.

She checked the mirror again, tilting her head to one side to see the rhinestones, and a flashbulb went off in her face. "Grandma, I *wish* you wouldn't do that!" Anne cried. Lights continued dancing in her eyes, making the queasy feeling come back.

"I always immortalize you before your dates," said her grandmother, paying no attention to Anne's complaints.

Panic began to crawl up Anne, like some kind of little slimy animal, taking control of her, walking on her skin.

She could hardly breathe.

The doorbell rang. Her mother and grandmother pounded down the stairs like two little kids, to let Con in. Grandmother got there first. She was a swim instructor at the Y and more athletic than any of them. Anne could hear Con's soft voice — very deep, very mellow. Everybody in school said it was the sexiest voice they'd ever heard. Anne would have to agree with that. Bellowing up the stairs to make her hurry, so he wouldn't have to talk to her mother and grandmother very long, Con shouted, "Anne! I'm here!"

"Coming," she called.

She thought, Maybe I could forget about it for a little while longer. Pretend. It's our first formal dance. This is my first formal gown. It's practically an historic event at the school, since it's been so long since they've allowed dances like this. Not since the vandalism three years ago. Who am I to ruin it for us?

She stared at the dress again.

She would never have chosen the dress herself. But she found her grandmother's decisions hard to argue with. The dress was rather too hard-edged, too sophisticated. Anne would have chosen something much softer, much more romantic. The dress was so bright it screamed.

Well, that's only right, she thought. I certainly feel like screaming. Perhaps I will scream. Go to the top of the stairs, look down at these three people who run my life entirely, and start screaming.

She walked to the top of the stairs, went down six steps to the landing, turned, and looked into the uptilted faces of the three people who admired her most in the world. Con was laughing, his wonderful smile spread across his face. He tossed the flowers up to her. Anne caught them and bent her face over the bouquet: gardenias. They smelled like paradise, thick with romance.

As she reached the bottom of the stairs, the flashbulb went off, but she was prepared this time, and kept her eyes focused on the lovely flowers. Tears came into her eyes again. "I love you, Con," she said huskily.

He looked faintly surprised. Was it because

he knew that already, and there was no reason to repeat it? Or was it because he didn't love her, loved only the good times he had with her, loved being the perfect couple with her, and. . . .

With all the self-control she had ever learned, Anne put a smile on her face. "Some dress!" said Con, which was high praise from him, and Grandmother Stephens looked happy.

"You'll be home by one A.M.?" her mother said to Con, frowning so that Con would know this was a command.

Con smiled. "Yes, we will." He put his arm around Anne.

"You do know there's a terrible storm out there," he said to her. "You got a raincoat or something?"

"A raincoat? Over *that* dress?" her grandmother said.

Anne's raincoat was shabby. She knew in the morning her mother would buy her a new one, having seen the shabbiness. "Let's run to the car, Con," she said, holding the coat over her to keep her hair dry.

She ran, and kept her hair dry. It reminded her of some old battle cry. *Keep your powder dry, boys.* If I tell him tonight, that's what tonight will be, thought Anne. A war zone. But I have to tell him tonight. I can't last alone any longer.

Con began driving.

He put the windshield wipers on high, and heavy rain flicked off the glass. Lightning tore through the sky, and thunder rolled. Anne stared at Con's profile. He didn't notice.

Chapter 3

Emily Edmundson hated thunder and lightning. She had read lots of statistics by now, and every time she had to leave the house during an electrical storm (or stay in the house alone) she reminded herself that few people were killed each year by lightning. Emily knew, however, that she was destined to be one of the few.

What would it be like to be burned to death by a shaft of electricity? Quick, at least.

Outside her bedroom window lightning fired in the sky like a series of warning signals. Don't go, don't go.

"Penny for your thoughts," said Emily's mother, fixing the hook at the top of the zipper in the back of Emily's dress.

Emily smiled tightly at her mother. But she didn't answer. Emily felt that she was boring. Therefore, all her thoughts were boring, too. Emily never knew what to do about being boring. Her life was dull, and apparently it was because she was a dull person. Right now Emily could not help thinking that her mother offered a penny for Emily's thoughts because that was all Mrs. Edmundson thought they were worth.

"I hope poor Matt recognizes you," said Emily's mother, laughing. "Goodness! The poor boy sat next to you in some assembly for an hour, and here he has to go out on a night like this to take you to a formal dance. We were all so surprised he agreed to go!"

Emily forced a smile. "Not as surprised as I was. Good thing I don't have any sisters for him to confuse me with. At least that way he'll know who the flowers are for."

Mrs. Edmundson patted Emily's arm and left her bedroom. Thunder rocked the foundations of the house. Emily, who kept track of such things, did not think she had seen such a fierce storm in years. And to think she had to leave her house, run through this wicked rain and lightning and thunder to get into Matt's car, and then do the very same thing again to get into the high school. And all the time pretending she hardly noticed. Because, as her mother would have been quick to reassure her, most people did not give lightning storms a thought.

Emily stared at herself in her mirror.

She could never tell if she was attractive or not. There were times when she felt the reflection in that mirror was quite satisfactory, and other times when she felt that leaving the house would be an act of cruelty to the general public who would have to look at her. But at last tonight she had the perfect dress. Old-fashioned, garnet-colored, the cloth was a heavy velvet. Very romantic, dark crimson, with the narrow-

est line of pearl beads around the swooping
neckline. She felt like the sort of girl who sat
with a feathered fan and flirted with the young
gentlemen.

Oh, how she wanted a lovely evening to go
with her lovely dress!

Her mother had certainly cooperated. Mrs.
Edmundson had taken Emily to the hairdresser,
and bought her earrings that looked as if they
had been custom made for the dress, with the
same narrow pearls, and even agreed to the
special purchase of matching shoes: shoes in
that dark romantic red that would never match
anything else in her life — shoes for a single
night.

Don't let it be a single night, prayed Emily,
staring at the sky. Let Matt fall in love with
me. Let this be the first night of many, many
more. Please.

She sighed.

The odds against such a thing were pretty
high.

She'd met Matt the second week of the term.
There was a regional student government conference. Nobody in Emily's school was interested in their own school government, let alone
a regional conference. Every class officer in
sophomore, junior, and senior year pleaded
conflict from sports, jobs, family, or lessons.
The social studies teacher in charge looked
vaguely around his Comparative Economics
class and said, "We have to send *somebody*.
Won't anybody volunteer to represent us?"

Emily raised her hand.

The teacher said (burning the words into Emily's mind as if printing them with a hot branding iron), "Oh, good. At least Westerly will have a warm body there."

That's all she was. A warm body. The teacher couldn't even remember her name. She had to spell Edmundson for him. And the next week when he demanded to know why she'd been absent from his class on Wednesday, she had to remind him about the conference.

But Matt had remembered. Emily called him up. The most daring thing she'd done in her life. She felt as if she were scaling Mount Everest just lifting that telephone. And Matt remembered. His laugh rang out over the phone as if Emily had made his day by calling.

"Emily!" he cried happily. "The only interesting person at that whole conference. It's great to hear your voice! So what's happening? Where are you calling me from? Are you up here? Are you coming our way? Want me to meet you at the turnpike exit?"

Emily was staggered. Her biggest fear had been thinking of something to say to him. And listen to this outpouring of interest! "I just called to talk," she said nervously. "I *would* drive up to see you if I had a driver's license though. And a car, and money to buy gas."

Matt laughed. "I'll settle for the phone call. It sounds like it could be a few years before you drive my way. Your timing is perfect. I'm doing trig. I hate math. Don't know why I'm planning to be an engineer when I hate math. You think maybe I should consider another career goal, Emily? What do you think about my becoming a disc jockey? I sure can talk."

Oh, yes, he could talk! For two hours they talked, and her mother didn't interrupt her once. They went over the conference, as if it really had been fun. But it was Matt who'd been fun. For once Emily had had good luck — sitting next to a strange boy in the auditorium who instantly introduced himself and informed her they would go to the lectures together, because a person could only survive this junk if he had an ally.

That was late September. All through October Emily thought about Matt.

Kip Elliott had created the Autumn Leaves Dance herself; chaired every committee, in her exuberance and determination to make it wonderful. Kip had a knack for publicity. Everybody in school — and Westerly had nearly 2,000 students — knew as each step was accomplished. And each time Emily heard about the next thing Kip had done for this dance, she thought, I wonder if Matt would. . . .

And over the phone he said, yes, he would, he'd love to.

And she believed him, because he was such a solid person; he seemed so trustworthy and good and funny. Like Con Winter, who dated Anne Stephens. Matt seemed perfect to Emily, so of course she believed him. She said it was formal and Matt said he had a tuxedo. She said her street was hard to find and Matt said he had the directions written down and would not lose them.

But he had not called her in the two weeks since then.

No flowers had been delivered.

He had done no double checking to be sure he had the right night, the right hour.

Emily turned out the light in her room, and stared into the pelting rain outside her window, and shivered when lightning ripped through the night. I'm a fool, she thought. He was just handing me a line. He didn't mean it. He won't come. A forty-five minute drive to Westerly in this weather? Next year's yearbook they'll have a new category. Biggest Jerk. Emily Edmundson. Most Gullible. Emily Edmundson.

The dance starts in fifteen minutes.

And he's not here.

Her mother walked into the room and flicked on the lights. "Don't sit in the dark, Emily. Honestly, Emily, this boy *will* come. Although I must admit if he doesn't show I'm going to be irritated."

Emily sat immovable in the garnet velvet dress, the pearls dangling delicately against her cheeks. Irritated? she thought. My mother will be irritated? I will be sick with shame and sadness and embarrassment and loneliness . . . and my mother will be irritated.

Emily sat alone.

Lightning flashed, thunder shuddered.

And Matt did not appear.

* * *

Molly Nelmes adored boys, and they adored her.

Sometimes she stared into her mirror, wondering what the boys saw. Certainly girls didn't see it. Molly didn't have a female friend in the world. Molly didn't have a great figure, either, or terrific looks, or wonderful hair. Yet she was the only girl who was truly in demand. She actually turned boys down fairly often, because she already had a date. Those same boys came back again, until she squeezed them into her schedule — or didn't squeeze them in, if they were duds.

But things had slacked off. All fall there had been nobody but Roddy. Over the summer, girls and boys had paired off. Molly hadn't run into this before; most of the boys at Westerly were pretty casual. Now they were imitating Anne and Con, who had been and remained the most tightly bound of couples.

Molly's favorite sweat shirt said SO MANY BOYS . . . SO LITTLE TIME. She had no intention of tying herself down to anybody.

Roddy was all right. A little on the thin and gawky side for her taste, but he'd fill out this year. He was seventeen, and even the shrimpy ones started growing when they hit seventeen. Not too bright, but brains weren't number one for Molly. Roddy had plenty of money, and she liked that. He could borrow his father's Jaguar, which she loved, and he had his own four-year-old Ford — not exciting, but there.

But Roddy had had the cars taken away. His grades fell, he got a speeding warning, he'd failed to write a thank you letter to his grandmother, or some dumb thing, and the cars had been taken away for six weeks.

As far as Molly was concerned, Roddy no longer had anything to offer. She herself had no car, and what good was a boy if he couldn't drive you to the movies or the Pou-Belle, or someplace? She especially liked the Pou-Belle. A coffeehouse/juice bar, with pool tables, darts, video games, wide screen television, and a dance floor. Pou-Belle meant "garbage can" in French, which appealed to Molly's sense of humor. She loved to hang out there.

They had ridden with another couple to Pou-Belle the week before and Roddy got all bent out of shape when Molly danced with other people. "I like to dance," she said to him. "And you're not good at fast dances. You just sort of stand there and twitch."

She was trying to be funny; she was laughing when she said it. But Roddy blushed an uncomfortable splotchy red, and mumbled, and fumbled. Molly couldn't stand being with a boy who was awkward. She walked away instantly, and who should be leaning against the bar, waiting for some action, but Christopher Vann.

She was amazed to see him. Christopher had graduated from Westerly High two years before. A sophomore at some Ivy League college back East, he was old enough now to drink legally. What on earth was he doing in a kids' juice bar? She went right up and asked him, in her direct way.

"Waiting for someone like you," said Christopher instantly, and Molly laughed, and forgot about Roddy. A few hours later when their ride was leaving, Roddy came up to her and Christopher. Looking down at his shoes (stupid shoes; shoes with Velcro pads instead of laces) he mumbled, "You ready to leave, Molly?"

"No," said Molly. "I'm going with Christopher."

Christopher grinned down at Roddy. Big, broad, and muscular, Christopher had been the football captain and president of his class as a senior. Almost got into West Point, but ended up at Harvard instead. Harvard. Molly adored the sound of it. *I go with a Harvard guy, of course,* she pictured herself saying.

"So what are you doing this weekend?" she said to Christopher.

Roddy shuffled a little bit. Molly thought, At least when you asked me to the Autumn Leaves Dance, you were a jerk with a Jaguar. Now you're just a jerk.

It would be fantastic to appear with Christopher. There were plenty of decent boys in Westerly now — like Con, or Gary—but Christopher was a Harvard man, and this year's crop was nothing like that. What a splash she would make, strolling in with Christopher! Molly was wildly excited.

"You got something in mind?" Christopher asked lazily.

"I'm taking you to a dance." She grinned at him mischievously, a grin she had long ago learned wrapped boys around her little finger.

Christopher fell right in line. "What kind of dance?" he said.

Roddy made a funny little sound.

Molly said, "Formal. At school. You've got to dust off your tuxedo and everything and I'll be wearing a dress cut so low you'll have trouble driving."

Christopher laughed. "Can't pass up an offer like that," he said. They talked about the dance and about Harvard, and what she would wear. Actually her dress wasn't that low cut because her mother wouldn't buy her anything like that, but Molly was no stickler for facts.

On Saturday night she was still laughing happily, without any memory of the way Roddy had slunk off and the way she and Christopher moved on to another nightclub— no juice bar this, but one where she had to lie about her age to get in.

What a catch Christopher was. Molly even thought of him that way — as something she had snagged, rather than a man she was with.

Boys, Molly thought contentedly. Her mirror told her the hairdresser had done her hair perfectly and her complexion was clear. I love boys, she thought. Girls, now. A dime a dozen. I hardly even notice girls. Except when they get in my way. But boys are worth counting one by one. I've never had a Harvard man before.

And what it would do for her status in school!

Not plain old Roddy, but Christopher Vann, who'd been Most Likely to Succeed and Best Dressed.

He'll invite me to a Cambridge weekend, she thought. Football. The Harvard-Yale game.

When the doorbell rang, and she heard Christopher's voice and her mother's, exchanging conventional greetings, Molly was almost delirious with pleasure.

It did not occur to her to wonder why a Harvard sophomore would be home for a week in November, with nothing better to do than go to a high school dance.

Chapter 4

"Mother," said Beth Rose, her voice tight with panic, "can you button me up?"

Unfortunately her mother's negative advice would come right along with the buttoning. But there was nobody else in the family to do it. She was an only child, and her father was a television addict who was even now glued to some Saturday night program, although at this hour there was nothing interesting on. Mr. Chapman never cared. He just watched, regardless.

Her mother walked into the bedroom and said, "Oh, honey, your hair looks awful. What are we going to do about it?"

Beth turned away quickly before the tears showed. Her mirror was not full length. It was a cheap rectangle from the discount store, sitting on top of her bureau, and the bottom was blocked anyway by all her rows of makeup and perfume. Bottles to make her beautiful. Bottles that had not lived up to their promise. And yet Beth Rose loved them all. She loved scents and colors. She made herself look at the mirror and knew that her mother was right. Her hair, which she had tried to fix the way Aunt Madge had, merely looked ridiculous. The braids were fat spikes that stuck out and the shining dark red cap of hair on top was frizzled and askew.

Her mother finished buttoning. "Let's leave," she said. "Now do you want me to wait outside the high school for you for fifteen minutes? I think that's the best thing, Bethie. If you get in there and you simply can't handle it, and nobody talks to you, you can just slip right out again and get in the car and we'll drive away and say no more about it. How does that sound?"

It sounded like a nightmare.

But it also sounded possible.

I'll walk in, thought Beth, and the gym will be perfect, because Kip was in charge. There will be beautiful corners and aisles of plants and clusters of seating arrangements and sparkling things hanging from the ceiling. I'll move like a stick figure from spot to spot, until I see and touch everything Kip designed and then I'll be back where I started from. And a few people will look at me pityingly, thinking, Does Beth Rose really think she can pull this off?

Oh, Aunt Madge, how could you do this to me! I really believed you were my fairy godmother, and you could wave your wand and make me beautiful and popular, but of course you aren't and you can't.

She didn't weep, but only because she was

used to things going wrong and her mother being negative.

Her father's voice came bellowing up the stairs. He disliked anything that interrupted his television. "Beth!"

"Yes, Daddy?"

"Your Aunt Madge is here. Come on down."

Aunt Madge? But she lived a hundred miles away!

Beth ran to the stairs, and the funny thing was, she instinctively knew to lift her skirt from the sides, ever so little, so that she didn't trip on the hem, and she held it gracefully, because the dress was so lovely it demanded grace. Aunt Madge was standing at the bottom with a heavy-set, middle-aged woman and they were both beaming. "Beth Rose!" cried Aunt Madge, clapping her hands. "I just had to come see how you looked. Didn't I tell you, Jeannette? Didn't I tell you she would be beautiful in my old prom dress?"

"You certainly did," said Jeannette, whoever she was. "And you were right. We got here just in time to fix her hair."

There were introductions. Jeannette was Aunt Madge's next door neighbor. This was a lark, they explained — an adventure in their quiet lives. They wanted to see the dress go out the door. "And how often do I get involved in a dance anymore?" added Aunt Madge.

She had Beth's messy braids out in an instant, and brush and comb flew through the hair so quickly it really felt like a magic wand.

Beth Rose kept laughing.

It was too wonderful. "I wish I'd known you were coming, Aunt Madge," she said happily.

"I didn't know myself. A hundred miles is a long way to come. But I've been thinking about your dance all day long and I couldn't bear it. It's my dress, you know. I went to my prom with Virgil Hopkinson. I worshipped Virgil Hopkinson. So did every girl in town. They were all jealous of me, Beth. I tell you, there's nothing so wonderful as a dance where every other girl in the ballroom is looking at you."

"But you didn't marry Virgil Hopkinson," said Beth.

"Oh, my, no. He wasn't worth marrying, darling. He just made a perfect escort. Tall, dark, handsome, and rich."

"I wonder what your life would be now if you had married him," said Beth Rose. Her hair was finished. She looked in the hall mirror, and the magical girl was back. The lovely fragile creature with the gleaming hair in her soft, old-fashioned dress, as if her edges had faded like an old photograph album, and she was drifting in from another world.

"Boring," said Aunt Madge. "Virgil was boring. People who travel on their looks often are. My dear, you are beautiful."

"And boring?" teased Beth.

"Never! Nobody could be bored with you around. Oooooh, I can't wait. I know you're going to have the best time of all," Madge said.

Her mother said nothing, but her eyebrows said it all. Mrs. Chapman was saying, "The best time? No. She'll arrive, she'll sit, and then she'll leave. That's the kind of time Bethie will have. That's the kind of time Bethie always has."

"Will you be staying for the night, Madge?" said Mrs. Chapman stiffly, giving the unknown Jeannette a false smile of welcome.

"No, no. We're driving right back. But it wouldn't be out of our way to drive Beth Rose to the high school," Aunt Madge said. "Why don't we do that for you, honey, and that will spare you having to go out alone in this dreadful weather."

"I'll still have to wait up for her," Mrs. Chapman complained.

Aunt Madge said, "A dance like this is worth a few hours of inconvenience." She looked in disgust at the light jacket Beth Rose was putting on. "A *jeans* jacket? With a *zipper*?"

"You make it sound obscene," said Beth.

"Next to my prom dress, it is." Aunt Madge frowned. "Don't you have a wrap? Some lovely wool stole? A felt blazer, even?"

Beth Rose shook her head.

Her mother said, "I do. I have that lace jacket that goes with one of my Sunday dresses."

Beth Rose almost fell over at the idea of her mother helping out, but Mrs. Chapman ran eagerly to her own closet and came back with a three-quarter-sleeve jacket. It was much too white for the dress; too stark, too obviously modern.

"But better than denim," said Aunt Madge, and Beth Rose put it on. "Just take it off the moment you're inside, dear," said Aunt Madge. "It'll give you something to do those first few moments, draping the jacket over your arm."

They went out the basement side door, slipping into the car without getting very wet because of the carport. The wind was fierce enough to throw the rain inside the carport anyhow, but Beth's dress stayed dry. Her Aunt Madge got into the front passenger seat and Beth slipped in back. Jeannette drove.

The rain came down in sheets, and the wind ripped into it like shears into fabric, slashing through the wetness, hurling it across the car violently. The car shuddered beneath the force of the wind. Trees on the sides of the road bent dangerously close to utility wires and Jeannette's fingers tightened into white knuckles on the steering wheel.

Beth Rose had no steering wheel to hang onto, but her knuckles were equally white.

They arrived at the high school. Huge overhead parking lot lights penetrated the dark and gloom in overlapping circles. Two cars ahead of them pulled slowly up to the front steps of the old portion of the school, whose pillars and granite towered like monuments to another age. A uniformed doorman materialized from the front doors, and dashed down the wet stairs, holding an enormous umbrella to hold over the couple getting out of some parent's car.

"How impressive," Aunt Madge said. "We never had a doorman when I was a girl."

"We never had a doorman when *I* was a girl, either," said Beth Rose. "He must be one of Kip's brainstorms. Hired for the occasion."

The first car pulled away. A beautiful couple

hunched beneath the umbrella scurried into the building. The doorman returned for the next couple.

Couples, thought Beth Rose. I'm alone. Nobody else will be alone. I can't do this! I can't go alone to a formal dance. This is crazy. "I can't go in, Aunt Madge," she whispered. Her chin began to tremble. If I cry, she thought, my eyes will turn red and my whole face will get all blotchy. I can't cry.

I'm going to cry.

Aunt Madge turned in her seat. "I love you, Bethie," she said in a soft voice. Beth Rose kissed the warm cheek. I love you, too, she thought, but she said nothing because she was afraid her voice would break.

I'm going to my execution, Beth Rose thought. A four-hour-long execution. True medieval torture. Witnessed by a paying crowd.

"Remember your dress," said Aunt Madge. "Remember you're an A-plus, not a C. Remember that I love you."

"I'll remember," Beth Rose croaked.

The doorman flung her door open and beamed at her. Water glistened on his gold braid decorations. "You look like Cinderella," said the doorman, smiling like a father or an uncle.

The aunts and uncles love me, thought Beth Rose, but that's what I have enough of. I need a boy age seventeen to love me!

She wanted to get back into the car, and turned to look once more at Aunt Madge, but her aunt was slumped against the seatbelt, tired by a long trip and a repeat drive ahead.

The doorman waited for a moment, frowning, expecting a boy to get out of the far side and join them. He looked oddly at Beth Rose who fibbed, "I'm meeting him here."

He believed her. His face cleared, he smiled, he took her arm and led her up seventeen steps to the door. It was like going to a guillotine. He opened the door for her, and went back down the stairs for the next couple. She was alone.

She stood very still.

A parent was standing in the foyer, smiling. Beth Rose gave her a stiff-lipped smile back. "Did your boyfriend go to park the car?" said the mother pleasantly. "Why don't you just wait here with me and then you can go in together. The photographer is taking pictures at the cafeteria door by the rose arbor, and you don't want to go in without him," she explained.

Beth shivered in the thin white inappropriate jacket.

"I came alone," she said.

The mother stared at her. The astonishment turned to pity. "Oh," said the mother awkwardly. "Oh, well then."

Beth Rose thought, I could just go stand in the bathroom for an hour before I call my mother.

Behind her the door opened again.

Anne and Con, the classic couple, walked in laughing.

Roddy MacDonald told his parents nothing, told his friends nothing, and most definitely told his sister nothing. Inside, his stomach churned and his head ached, but outwardly he did the required homework to bring his grades back up, and wrote a thank you and an apology to his grandmother, and washed his father's car in the hope this would soften his parents' stand a little. It didn't. He was still without wheels for six long weeks. Thursday and Friday in school were torture.

People talked about the dance. Mostly the girls talked about it, but the guys mentioned it a little. You knew who was going, who was not. They assumed Roddy was taking Molly.

What was he supposed to say? "No. She had a better offer."

"No. She dumped me and asked somebody better."

He just said nothing.

Nobody actually questioned him. A lot of the boys routinely said nothing about their girls, or lack of girls. It was his business. Or it would be till Saturday night, when people would begin arriving at the dance. They'd see Molly with Christopher Vann. And he, Roddy, wouldn't be there. He'd be home, moping. Feeling sick and inadequate and thin and stupid and. . . .

Roddy tried not to think how worthless he was.

Saturday, all day long, his thoughts were on the dance. He'd gone with his mother to rent the tux. It was in his closet. Flowers had been ordered the week before that. He was going to have to pay for them, anyway. He worked Monday and Tuesday afternoons and evenings at the gas station. He thought of last week, when it rained and was cold, like tonight. He'd dashed in and out, checking oil, filling gas tanks, scrubbing filthy windshields, earning money for the evening with Molly.

Aaaaaahh. Christopher was going to have some forum in which to show off. All the kids who had been little freshmen and sophomores when he was a big splashy important Number One Senior were juniors and seniors themselves now. Christopher would be swaggering, impressive Ivy League, Molly on his arm. He'd be big man on two campuses that night.

For once, Anne and Con wouldn't be Couple Number One. Molly and Christopher would give them a run for their money.

His mother called down the hall, "Roddy, dear, shouldn't you be getting ready for the dance?"

"Okay, Mom," he said. He went into the bathroom to take a shower as if he really intended to go to the dance.

Outside the sky groaned, thunder splitting his thoughts like the sounds of war. Lightning whipped across the black sky. Roddy pulled the shade down.

Kip isn't going, he thought. I've always liked Kip. It's her dance and she didn't get invited to go. I wonder if. . . .

No.

Impossible.

He turned on the water and held his finger under it to test the temperature. He thought, Right now. Quick. Before I lose the courage. I'll call Kip.

He wrapped a towel around his waist, went into his room, looked up her phone number, and dialed, all in thirty seconds. His stomach began to hurt as if lightning had struck him and burned through. Acid. He swallowed. He thought, I can't believe I'm doing this. One hour until the dance and I'm calling a girl up? I'm worse than Molly.

He said, "Hi, Kip? It's Roddy."

There was a blank pause.

"Roddy MacDonald," he said helplessly, knowing that his first name alone had meant nothing to her. Now he really felt sick. He was calling up some girl who didn't even *know* him. Didn't *want* to know him. If he hadn't given her his last name he would have hung up. Now he clung to the telephone and struggled to think of an intelligible sentence. None came to mind.

Maybe I should just throw myself down the cellar stairs and be done with it, Roddy thought. He said, "Would you like to go to the dance with me tonight, Kip?"

Kip Elliott lived on the seventh floor of a luxury apartment building high on the city's only hill, overlooking the entire town. On clear days you could see past the newest housing developments, with their neatly spaced yards and tiny new trees, and on beyond to the last lingering farms and woods. At night from the dining room table they looked out on dancing streetlights and the soft trajectories of headlights.

Tonight the darkening sky throbbed with the fire of an electrical storm.

Fits my mood perfectly, Kip thought. She pushed her pot roast around in the gravy, making little dams with her mashed potatoes. The rest of the family watched her unhappily. Kip was the oldest of five and was supposed to set good examples. Tonight she was a failure. They were all witnesses to it. She could fake things in front of the kids at school, and she would be absent from the scene of her failure tonight whether she liked it or not — but her family Kip could not avoid.

"Now the important thing," said her thirteen-year-old brother, "is not to think of yourself as a complete zero. I mean, so nobody wanted to ask you to the dance. It's only a dance. It's not that big a thing."

"Thank you, George," said Kip. "I feel a hundred times better now."

"How come you just don't go, anyway?" piped her ten-year-old brother. "Don't you want to see the dance with everybody there dancing?"

All her brothers had helped with the decorations. They'd built the rose arbor under which the couples' photographs would be taken; they'd hauled in the barrels, and the bales of hay, and the bushels of apples, and the piles of pumpkins that were some of the props for her Autumn Leaves Dance.

"Why would I want to see that?" snapped Kip.

"Well, you did chair the whole dance," said the ten-year-old, as if she might have forgotten. "You did work for a whole month getting the cafeteria ready to be a ballroom. And we worked on it, too." His whole face lit up. He looked angelic when he was excited. "I know, Kippie!" he cried. "You and I will go! Then we both get to see how it looks in the dark with people there!"

"Get lost," said Kip.

"Really, Katharine," said her mother sternly. "Don't yell at your brothers just because you are having a difficult time. They have done their very best for you."

Kip said nothing. She cleared her place and took temporary refuge in the kitchen, where there were no brothers lurking. At least she could be sure nobody would come in the kitchen without being forced; they were a family that loved cooking and hated cleaning up.

She scraped her plate into the garbage disposal. Every other girl in Westerly is getting ready for my dance, she thought. They're not doing dishes. They're putting on new eye shadow. Fixing their hair. Getting ready for the best night of their lives.

So I chaired the dance. Big deal. I can decorate. I can locate a good band. I can hire the off-duty policemen and round up chaperones and sell tickets and get door prizes donated and rent a spiffy uniform for a hired doorman.

I can't attract a boy.

What's the matter with me?

How can I have so many friends in school and be so happy all day long and never have a boy really like me?

Her life had fallen into a pattern that made her want to scream or weep. When the sun was out, her life was filled with laughter and talk and school and friends and activities. At home she had four brothers and ate supper and did her homework, and she didn't mind any of that.

But about eight-thirty, every single night, she finished her homework. And wondered if maybe tonight the phone would ring.

Monday. Good time for a boy to call just to talk.

Tuesday. Perfect night to call to ask her out for Saturday.

Wednesday. Still time.

And of course by Thursday night, as she lay awake, long, long after eight-thirty, she had to acknowledge that yet another week had passed, and she, Kip Elliott, was still not good enough to enter a boy's mind when he wanted a girl to go out with him.

Every single girl she knew well had a date for the dance. Sure, some of the dates were duds — but at least somebody wanted to be with them. Not even the duds wanted to be with Kip.

She thought, as she so often did, of Anne Stephens and Conrad Winter. What a storybook couple. They even looked like the bride and groom on the wedding cake. They were always together. They were exactly the same height. Their eyes were always level, always locked. When they daydreamed, they were staring at each other, so that they seemed quite literally to be on the same wavelength.

The perfect posture, thought Kip.

And I don't know what it feels like.

And maybe I never will.

Perhaps she was doomed never even to know what a *kiss* was, let alone love and sex.

We had to take sex education classes, Kip thought, loading the dishwasher. The school was all worried that we'd be promiscuous, and I can't even get a voice on the telephone! They didn't need to lecture *me* on anything.

Desolation so immense it was greater than the thunder that rolled around the apartment building settled on Kip's heart. It was a despair too great for tears. A sense of failure beyond anything she had ever known.

She tried to tell herself it was just a dance. But it wasn't true. This was *her* dance. She had wanted it; she had lobbied for it, she had created it. She had sold it.

It was the first formal dance in over three years. The last time a bunch of rowdy kids got into a bathroom and broke a fixture; water leaked out behind the rear wall and nobody knew it, and this little bit of vandalism cost the school over thirty thousand dollars, because the entire gymnasium floor, with its expensive slick wood, had to be replaced after who knew how many gallons of water settled on it over the weekend.

It was Kip who convinced the administration to let her have a dance, and it was Kip who promised they would have no vandalism because they were such a splendid bunch of kids.

Splendid, thought Kip bitterly. Oh yeah, I'm really splendid.

Dance.

I don't even know how to dance with a boy.

I dance in my own room to the radio. How would it feel to have a boy's arms around me?

"Phone for you, Kippie," said her littlest brother. Jamie was four. He drove them all crazy. He was the kind of kid where you wondered how he would reach adulthood, with three brothers and a sister planning homicide every time they were near him. Kip was willing to bet there was no phone call, and if there was, it wasn't for her. Jamie always got phone calls wrong.

The phone was in the living room. Where her entire family was now stretched out on couches and the floor, arguing about whether to see an old movie on the VCR or watch a rerun of something else on tv.

"Hello," said Kip to the phone. It's going to be some other loser, she thought. Some girl sitting home alone and unwanted. We'll have some horrible depressing conversation. By the time we're done I'll be so depressed I'll want to sit in a closed garage with the exhaust running.

"Hi, Kip," said a boy's voice. "It's Roddy."

Roddy? She didn't know anybody named Roddy.

"Roddy MacDonald," the voice said eventually.

Roddy MacDonald. A boy to whom Kip could safely say she had never given a single thought. He was tall. Did he have anything else going for him? She didn't think they had ever shared a class or a lunch period; she knew they'd gone to different junior highs. "Hello, Roddy," she said. Must be something wrong at the high school, she thought. He probably expects me to correct it. That's me. Good old reliable Kip. She's boring but she works hard.

"Listen," Roddy said in a bright, rather silly voice. "I know it's real late, and all, but I all of a sudden felt like going to the dance after all. I didn't want to before today and I've been thinking about it all day and I heard them saying you didn't have a date. You want to come with me?"

He heard them saying? Kip thought, her stomach wrenching with humiliation. Who is them? What were they saying?

Oh, poor Kip, here she organized the whole thing and she's the only one without a date. . . . Well, what do you expect from a loser like Kip?

She thought she could not bear it, a nobody like Roddy MacDonald calling to tell her local gossip had it she wasn't worth a date. "It's seven-thirty," she said drearily. "The dance is at eight."

"Yeah. I have a tux. You must have a dress. Want to?"

She scarcely knew Roddy. Go to her formal dance with someone who could be El Creepo? But he could be Mr. Right, too. Kip made a face. Roddy was Mr. Nothing, as far as evidence showed.

Go to the dance after all. Her dance. She tried to weigh the pros and cons. Would it be more humiliating going with Roddy or not going at all?

I don't want life to do this to me! she cried out against the fate she had drawn. I don't want to decide between two humiliating things! I want love and romance just like everybody else! Out loud, she said, "I guess I have a dress."

Her mother almost fell off the recliner arm where she was perched. "Yes, you do!" she mouthed, signaling frantically. "That dress we picked up two months ago! When you first started planning the dance and we thought of course you'd — well, you know — uh — " Her mother's voice drifted off, unable to find an easy finish.

Kip had left the dress in its bag and stuck it so far in the back of her closet she had actually forgotten about it. Why remember a dress you weren't going to wear? Actually the dress was too summery for a dreadful night like this — a stab of winter the first week in November. But it was formal, it was pretty, and it was there.

Mentally she pulled straws from a clenched fist to make the decision for her. "Okay," she said, shrugging. "What time will you be here, Roddy?"

There was a silence. She heard him breathe in very heavily. "Uh," said Roddy. "Well, see, um. . . ."

Her little brother Jamie rolled over onto her feet and began twisting up the telephone cord. She smacked him with it and he began to cry. I know how you feel, Kip thought. Life is always hitting me for no reason, too.

"Can you drive?" Roddy said, sounding defeated. "I — uh — I got a speeding ticket last week and my father grounded me."

I have to drive my own loser to my own dance,

she thought. I believe it. It's my life in a nut-shell. "I'll get you at eight-thirty," she said.

At least her mother was excited. Mrs. Elliott was up like a shot, screaming, "Gloves! Coat! Somebody heat up the iron! Jamie! Plug in my electric curlers!"

George, Kevin, Jamie, and Pete got up to obey their mother. In the Elliott family you did what you were told or you repented for weeks on end.

Kevin said to Kip, "Somebody actually asked you out? Gosh."

He turned to George. "Well, I lose the bet, then. I'll get you your dollar."

"I'll kill you both!" screamed Kip, leaping for them.

The boys laughed.

Mrs. Elliott said, "Katharine, you'll do nothing of the kind. Stand still while I fix your hair."

"Is this romance?" demanded Kip. "Is this the way it ought to be?"

"No, but it's better than nothing," said her mother.

I don't want to be better than nothing. Better than nothing is lousy! Kip thought. I want to be a ten. A star.

But George was getting out the ironing board, and Pete was bringing the dress, and now she remembered what it looked like, and actually it was very pretty, a good color: dark peach, flushed like the petals of a rose, and suddenly Kip felt pretty good. After all, it might be her night.

Chapter 5

"Okay," whispered Emily to the thunderous night, "okay, he's not coming. Half an hour late, no phone call. That's pretty certain."

She did not cry. There would be plenty of time later in the evening for sobbing. The important thing now was not to cry in front of her mother. Her mother believed in Spine and Backbone and in Not Yielding to Self-Pity.

Why did I call him? she thought. It's not the end of the world to miss a dance. Look at Kip. Nobody is more interesting or more fun than Kip, and nobody asked her. And *she* didn't cast around trying to find somebody from out of town to make up the gap. She didn't need to humiliate herself like that. Why did *I* do it?

For a moment her thoughts stuck on Kip. How a thousand boys could look at Kip and not want to go out with her was beyond Emily. Just went to show how stupid boys could be.

Emily's throat hurt. I'm getting the flu, she thought. But she knew she wasn't. It was depression, seizing her like a strangler.

Out in her yard the lightning changed texture and shape. It stood still, thickly spreading itself like yellow mist. Emily's throat closed in fear and she momentarily forgot Matt and the dance. *What was out there?*

Her mother's voice wafted up the stairs and through her closed door. "Emily," she called. "I think he's finally arrived."

Car headlights. Trying without much success to pierce the driving rain. Inside her head she was screaming with delight, He came! He's here! I'm going after all! Her exterior was perfectly calm. She walked firmly to her bedroom door, casually to the top of the stairs, and then, unable to contain herself longer, raced down, and flung open the front door like a kindergartner waiting for party guests.

In the driveway sat a very old-fashioned car. Perhaps fifty or sixty years old, it had running boards, shiny brass fittings, and tall old-fashioned wiper blades that moved in a stately way over a nearly vertical windshield.

The driver's door opened. A dark figure hunched down and sped toward her, slipping on the flagstone steps, catching himself and taking all four porch steps in one great boyish bound. She held the door, pressing herself against it to give him room, and when he was in, and she had pulled the door and latched it against the force of the wind, she looked into the face of Matt O'Connor and got the shock of her life.

Matt O'Connor was the best-looking boy she had ever seen. Even better-looking than Con. Thick straight black hair ran with water. Matt shook his head like a puppy. A big goofy grin covered his whole face; his eyebrows lowered, his eyes crinkled nearly shut, and his lashes were squashed to nothing. The grin diminished slightly, and became more mature, and then it faded, and before her — very wet — stood an old-fashioned illustration of Total Happiness.

But I always know whether a boy is cute, thought Emily. She kissed him spontaneously, and it was easy, and it was fun, and neither of her parents commented. I rate all boys on a scale of ten, thought Emily. And here I sat with this boy for five hours, laughing like mad the whole time, and I forgot to rate him. The one boy I've ever asked out — I didn't give him a rating. I believe he could be a nine point five. He is *darling*.

"I kept getting lost," Matt said. "You told me your house would be hard to find, but you forgot to say that tonight you planned to have electrical wires down so I'd have to take a detour." He produced a massive black umbrella, which he held out for Emily to take. It was closed.

She giggled. "Maybe you'd be drier if you opened it," she suggested.

He shook his head. "Umbrella's for you. That's because I'm so gallant. Your dress is great. My mom said I had to bring white flowers because I was too stupid to ask what color your dress is, so we're all set. They sure are smelly. Gardenias. Mom said gardenias are perfect and only a jerk would call them smelly." He laughed.

The laugh spread over his face again and she watched in delight as the dark features crinkled closed, relaxed, and returned to position.

"*Your* mother calls you stupid?" she said.

"Sure. I never pay any attention to her. Listen, we're late. We gotta get going."

Emily marveled. Maybe a lot of parents said things like that and other people just shrugged. She would have to try shrugging. It certainly worked for Matt.

Emily's father stood at the glass storm door and stared almost reverently at Matt's car. "What year is that?" he asked Matt. "Nineteen twenty-eight? Thirty?"

"Nineteen thirty-two Ford," Matt said proudly. "First year they had a V-8 engine."

"Is it yours?" said Mr. Edmundson, as if he could not bear to think that a seventeen-year-old boy would possess a car like that.

"Of course not," Matt said, laughing. "It's my grandfather's. He collects old cars. Always has. He said for a formal dance I could borrow it. If anything happens to it, he'll kill me, so you don't have to worry about Emily, Mr. Edmundson. We'll be the most cautious drivers in the entire state, because when my grandfather kills a person, it's for good."

Matt had a capacity to sound like a nut and yet like the most sane person in the room. Emily felt herself falling in love with him. She let herself fall. It was like tipping over, and being caught in the net of Matt's presence.

Matt turned to Mr. Edmundson. "When do we

have to be home?" he asked. To Emily he said, "My mother says she'll kill me if I break your parents' rules."

"You people certainly go in for murder," observed Emily's father, but he was grinning. He's impressed by Matt, Emily thought. And when her father went and got her coat, and held it for her like a gentleman, she realized something even more surprising. He was impressed with her — his own daughter. It took Matt to accomplish it. Emily felt a brief flicker of resentment, but there was no time to think about it, because Matt was opening the door for her to run to the car.

"Actually," said Matt, "the wind's blowing too hard to open the umbrella. It'll turn inside out and be ruined and then I'll be in trouble for that, too."

"Oh, no," she giggled. "Your family kills over umbrellas, too?"

"Sure. Listen, just pull your coat over your hair and we'll run."

They ran.

Matt jerked the passenger door open and helped her in. The car was much higher off the ground than anything she'd ever ridden in, and it surprised her to have to climb up to get in. Matt raced around, slipping in a puddle but not falling down, and flung himself in next to her. They sat laughing, dripping, and shivering.

"Whew," said Matt. "I'm soaked. We'll take a long slow route to get to the high school so I can dry off a little. Otherwise I won't make a good impression on your friends."

Emily burst out laughing. How incredible that *Matt* could worry about making a good impression. What other impression was he capable of? "Everybody'll be just as wet," she pointed out. She touched her own hair. "Oh, it's soaked, too," she wailed.

Matt looked confused. "Your hair is perfect," he said, hardly glancing at it, and he started the engine.

The seats in the 1932 Ford were leather, and very cold. The cold seeped through Emily's thin coat and her dress to her skin and she shivered. "Slide over against me," said Matt. "Body heat does wonders, you know?"

Emily did not know. But she knew she wanted to find out, so she slid over and sat next to him.

"This car doesn't have seat belts, Emily. My grandfather got all uptight about us driving because he thinks it's dangerous. I had to promise nine hundred times to drive carefully. But just don't forget if we do have an accident that there's nothing hanging onto you."

Matt smelled of wet wool. Like sweaters and mittens. What could he be wearing that had such a distinctive scent?

Lightning leaped ahead of them, thunder following it so quickly and so loudly that it drowned out Matt's next sentence. Emily closed her eyes and shivered in spite of all efforts to stop herself.

"You don't like lightning?" said Matt.

"I hate it."

"I love it when the thunder makes everything tremble. Primitive," said Matt. "Strong. Wild."

"It's going to kill me someday," Emily told him. "I feel it in my bones."

"Not in my car," said Matt, patting her knee, and then leaving his hand there, warming her through the velvet, and making her tremble with something other than fear of lightning. "The only thing you have to worry about is the distance between the car and the high school front door," he said. He began teasing her about her destiny. "Maybe you have a rendezvous with lightning on the school steps," he kidded.

"Don't even joke about it. It's not funny to me. It makes me sick inside to think about lightning. I'm not sure how afraid of lightning I am, on a scale of afraid-ness, but I think I fall into the category of phobic on lightning."

"I kid about everything," Matt told her. "Don't worry, Emily. I can't have you roasted before the dance. Who'll I dance with then?"

They both laughed.

"You look beautiful," Con said softly.

Anne looked at him in the dark of the car. Streetlights swept shadows over and across his face, and as he turned to smile at her, his features were unknown and mysterious. She could just barely keep from crying. "Thank you." She thought, Did Mother prime him? Or is he learning at last?

Maybe it really is *at last*, she thought.

Con took her hand. "You're freezing," he said. He turned up the heat and redirected all the vents so that warm air poured over her. "Have to take care of my girl," he said, grinning sideways. He drove with one hand, something she hated because it was dangerous . . . and yet loved, also because it was dangerous.

Maybe that's why I like sex, she thought. Danger.

They arrived at the high school.

In one great, eerie flash lightning illuminated the building. Three stories high, brick, with white columns set into the brick over the wide granite steps. A storybook high school, with its modern expansion safely hidden out back. I love the building, Anne Stephens thought. It's my life. And this is autumn of my junior year. What about senior year, what about . . . .

"We're here," said Con unnecessarily. He leaned over and kissed her and in his eyes she could see his love: It was there, clear and true. "I knew you'd look great in that dress," he said, "but I didn't know you'd look this great."

His words came awkwardly. She knew they were his own, not her mother's tutoring.

Now, Anne thought. Now when I can see that he loves me. She cleared her throat. "Con?" she said.

"Yes. Here's the doorman. You go inside under his umbrella; I'll park the car and be in in five minutes." Con undid her seatbelt, the doorman opened the door and took her arm. She was out of the car, on the doorman's arm, and Con had driven off.

With a grand motion that matched the sweep of his mustache, the doorman graciously helped Anne over the puddles and up the wide shallow steps into the foyer. No, no, no! she thought.

Drive me home! I want to go home. I want to be my mother's little girl and have nothing to do but line up my Barbie dolls in their Barbie playhouse. I want to be Anne the perfect daughter, Anne, the perfect granddaughter. I don't want —

But they were in the school.

It smelled like school. No matter what Kip did, the smell of school would never leave these halls. People and books, sweaty gym socks and leaking pens, clean paper and illicit smoking.

The doorman left her for the next car.

She had never felt so out of control. She felt papery, as if she could be crumpled and tossed away without effort.

The doorman brought Molly in.

"Ooooh, Anne," squealed Molly. "You look absolutely *lovely*. I adore your dress."

With tremendous effort Anne said, "Thank you, Molly. You look lovely, too." It sounded fake, it was fake, and Molly knew it. She maintained courtesy, but Anne knew with a sinking heart that Molly would be difficult all night. Molly had a real ability to damage people. Boys never seemed to notice, but then, as she knew to her cost, boys were thicker than cement all the time, anyway. Molly's eyes narrowed, and her laugh turned spiteful. Anne turned away and studied the wall, and in that moment made her fatal mistake.

Turn away from me? Molly thought with concealed rage. Pretend I'm not standing here, when we're the only two people in this entire foyer? Who do you think you are, Anne Stephens?

The doors were flung open, both at the same time, and two boys entered, without the doorman.

Con. Perfect. Grinning at her. Rain running off his hair. She could not move toward him.

Molly went instantly to her date and snuggled against him in spite of the rain. Con's eyes rested on Molly for several seconds. Before he walked to Anne he said, "Hello, Molly. Evening, Christopher."

Christopher Vann, that's who her date was! Anne remembered him now. Two years ago he'd been everything. Football captain, soccer co-captain, basketball guard, the whole jock career. Christopher was at Harvard now. For Molly he had flown home to go to a high school dance? Wow.

Christopher put out a hand to shake with Con and Anne knew instantly that Christopher was drunk. Don't get involved with them, Con, she thought, horrified. Vividly she remembered that Christopher could get rough. He was always the first to foul out in a game, the first to start a fight, the first to swear . . . and the last to stop.

She walked up to Christopher, Molly, and Con, and took Con's arm to turn him toward her.

Molly's long lashes followed this gesture and Molly laughed, and Con and Anne could read the laugh as if it were the page of a book —

What's the matter, Anne? Afraid Con's too interested in me?

"Let's go on in and see Kip's decorations," said Anne in a brittle, bright voice.

Con went with her. "What's the matter with you?" he said, faintly irritable. "You weren't exactly friendly to them."

"I don't exactly like them."

"Oh, that's a great attitude to start the evening with, Anne," said Con. "Now listen, if you can't be cheerful, forget it. You've been moody for days. It's getting on my nerves."

Anne trembled. Ahead of them Molly wrapped herself around Christopher and they swayed from side to side, dancing to inaudible music, or perhaps holding each other up. Behind them somebody else walked. Anne could hear the sound of the dress rustling, but lacked the curiosity to turn to see who it was.

With the worst possible timing, at the worst possible moment Anne whispered, "I'm not moody, Con. I'm pregnant."

Chapter 6

There should be a rule, Kip thought. Never drive a car that has manual transmission while wearing a floor-length gown.

Her gleaming satin slippers were pressed where usually only dirty sneakers lay. She had had to yank up the ruffles of peach and rose around her knees to keep it off the floor. The unused bottoms of her slippers slithered over the brakes ineffectually.

I can't believe I'm driving, Kip thought. And of course Roddy lives in a subdivision still under construction. Of course I have to drive over sewer pipe bumps and around lanterns I can barely see in the rain, and of course he said, "Oh, my house is easy to find, it's the gray one," and of course it's dark and every single house in the whole stupid neighborhood looks gray.

She saw Roddy by the side of the road. He was wearing a raincoat and holding a newspaper over his head. The newspaper was drenched and flattened into pulp that drooped onto his hair.

Great, Kip thought. I'm going to the dance with a wet nerd. Just what I've always yearned to do. "Well, for heaven's sake, get in!" she shrieked over the thunder. "Who do you think it is in this car?" she muttered more quietly. "Santa Claus?"

Roddy got in, soaking her upholstery, like a kid from the beach who forgot his towel. He wasn't quite so dull-looking as she remembered. In fact he was okay-looking. Just very wet. "Hi, Roddy," she said tonelessly. She was desperately regretting her decision to go with him, but fatalism had set in. She was in motion now, there was no stopping the events to come, and if she were meant to suffer total humiliation in front of every person she knew or cared about, so be it.

Roddy said, "Hi, Kip. Thanks a lot for coming. Do you mind turning the heat up a little? I'm kind of chilled. I thought you'd be here quicker."

I hate boys who get cold and chilled, she thought. I like boys who show up in January wearing sleeveless sweat shirts, complaining they're suffering of heat prostration.

She turned up the heat. Roddy put his hands in front of the vents, shivered noticeably, and said, "Gee, we're going to have fun, aren't we?"

Kip lived by certain rules. One that she never broke was that if she intended to do something anyway, she would do it courteously and to the best of her ability.

Now it struck her as a very stupid rule. Why should she have this stupid date with a smile?

Why should she work hard to make the evening pleasant? She *always* worked hard, and where did it get her? Nowhere. Roddy was the jerk who'd called and she was the jerk who'd said yes. Let it all go down the tubes. She didn't care.

She said nothing to him.

Roddy looked at her nervously. She hated nervous people. She liked solid secure people who got things done.

Silently they crossed Westerly, paying no attention to the storm or their surroundings, saying nothing, Kip caught in her bitterness, Roddy caught in his embarrassment.

Con said flatly, "Don't be ridiculous."

He kept right on walking. Molly and Christopher were the same distance ahead, and whoever was behind them was the same distance behind. It had never crossed Anne's mind that Con would simply dismiss the idea of her being pregnant. "But Con . . ." she said. Doubt and hope entered Anne in spite of herself. Maybe it was ridiculous. Maybe the tests had been wrong. Maybe she should go to another doctor.

"We always used stuff," said Con impatiently. He detested the real names of any contraceptives. *Stuff* was his word. "Let's not ruin a perfectly nice evening. You *aren't*. Okay?"

Anne came to a halt. "Except sometimes we didn't bother," she said.

Con's eyes found a spot on the wall above and to the left of her.

"Don't look at me," he said, not looking at her.

She was filled with rage and terror, but even

61

more with a dreadful need to placate him. He mustn't get mad at her. She needed him. "Okay," she said, "this is the wrong time. But Con, there *is* no time. We — we have to — talk — about — about — "

She couldn't say the real words, either. Words like baby, illegitimate, childbirth, abortion, adoption, marriage — all those caught, snagged by fear, and didn't come out of her mouth. "Stuff," she said lamely.

Con put his arm around her waist and began walking again. She could not believe it. In a moment they would have caught up to Molly and Christopher. "Con," she whispered.

His fingers tightened painfully around her. His lips came right to her ear, as if he were nuzzling her lovingly. "I could kill you for bringing this up now. Don't you dare do it again," he hissed.

She was so cold now her back ached.

Molly's rich laugh rang out. "No, no, you guys. The way it works is, you walk *inside*, and kiss under Kip's little rose arbor, and get immortalized on film."

"Expensive film," added Christopher.

"Oh, is that how it works," said Con, laughing.

Anne struggled to laugh with him. Nothing came to her face but fear and anger, and that she could not show. She kept it blank instead, and again she saw Molly's expression — *Oh, Anne won't laugh with me, huh?* said Molly's vivid features.

Anne looked at Con. This is my fault, she

thought. Any girl with half a brain would have planned this conversation better. I —

And then she thought, Now wait a minute. He's the father. He should have planned a little better. Who is he to complain? Is *he* pregnant?

"Poor Kip," said Molly. "She did such a nice job on decorations and nobody asked her to her own dance. Isn't that sad?"

You stinker, Anne thought. You haven't even seen the decorations yet. You just want to announce somebody's bad luck and jeer at somebody who's not here to defend herself.

"Kip doesn't have a date?" repeated Con, visibly amazed.

Now the coldness shivered up Anne's spine, settling in her skull, throbbing like a glacial headache. He likes Kip. If he leaves me, will he turn around the next night and call another girl? Kip, say? Could Con do that — after three years with me?

Con was not looking at Anne. He walked her into the gym, and they were, and she knew it, the picture of romance. A kneeling photographer caught them, bulb flashing. Con was laughing, pressing his cheek against hers, looking right into the flash.

He won't look at me again, she realized. That might make it real. He'll get through this entire evening without letting it get real.

She stared at the cafeteria and knew in a moment that Con could pull it off. Because Kip had succeeded beyond anybody's wildest dreams. The cafeteria was no longer real: It was a fantasy of fallen leaves and shining stars.

Hundreds of brilliantly colored autumn leaves hung from invisible wires strung across the ceiling. An actual fountain splashed gently on rocks. Behind it greenery formed a wreath for two benches. Already coins twinkled in the water where couples had made wishes. If a penny would make my wish come true, Anne thought ruefully, I'd sit all night by that fountain.

Baskets of flowers, stacked pumpkins, and split rail fences flanked a scarlet runner that led to a barnboard refreshment stand. Behind bales of hay, junior high girls dressed in white lace and black cotton maid costumes were serving cider and wedges of apple pie. A wheelbarrow piled high with real autumn leaves stood next to an old wooden porch swing.

Beyond lay the dance floor.

No d.j. for this dance! A live band, dressed in Anne's colors: electric screaming royal blue, threaded with silver, flashing with rhinestones, instruments gleaming in the musicians' hands. The drummer nodded hypnotically over his drums. The singer's mouth was wed to his mike.

Above them were no autumn leaves. The ceiling was hung with stars of mylar, and the lighting pointed up and the stars glistened. A break in the forest . . . a setting for romance.

Anne and Con were instantly the center of action. For the first time Anne realized that it was Con who attracted the groups of kids, not herself. She was not participating; she simply stood there while Con hugged her waist, tugging her close, releasing her, tugging her close again, at whatever beat the drummer set.

She was terribly aware that all these people saying hello, and laughing, and clapping Con on the shoulder were *his* friends, or perhaps *their* friends, but none of them were *her* friends. Oh, Con, she thought, choking with fear, oh Con, don't be mad at me, don't leave me, I have no one else, I can't go home and face my mother and my grandmother without you, *oh, Con, please* . . . .

Into her hair Con whispered, *"Smile."*

She smiled. She said the right things. She even managed to laugh at the appropriate moments. I'm pregnant, she thought at them. What would you do if I told you that? Would you laugh like Con? Would you say, don't be ridiculous, Anne, you're perfect, you don't do things like that?

Maybe that's what people normally do when somebody tells them something they don't want to hear, Anne thought. What would I say in Con's place? If he said to me, *Your father's dead. Your house burned down. Your country is at war.* Would I say, *Don't be ridiculous, Con. Stop trying to ruin my evening.*

"If I know Kip," said Con, "there's enough food for an army tonight. Let's go pig out."

She could barely talk, let alone swallow food. She nodded brightly, and a whole crowd of them headed for the scarlet path. Kip's arrangement forced them to walk only two abreast, and they marched, like soldiers, headed for food. Everybody joked.

Not one person noticed anything wrong with

Anne. She had never been so aware that she was merely Con's girl, not Anne Stephens. As long as Con laughed, they would just assume she was laughing, too. They would never really look to see.

Never in her life had Beth Rose Chapman done anything so difficult as walk down that corridor after Anne and Con. The closeness of them! The way Con had his arm around her. The way he paused to brush his lips over her burnished gold hair and whispered lovingly.

Beth's heart hurt. I don't have that kind of love, she thought. Did I think I was going to come here and find it waiting for me, like a package on layaway?

She could hide out in the lavatory for two hours, telephone home, fib about the dance.

"After you," said a gallant male voice, and Con laughed and took Anne ahead of another couple. Beth Rose drew inexorably nearer. The other couple were Molly and some older, handsome, wonderful-looking guy.

"What a beautiful dress!" exclaimed Molly, as Beth Rose came up to them.

Molly, who could get boys the way Beth could get ducks when she flung stale bread into the pond. "Here, duck, duck, duck," Beth would call, and the ducks came. "Here, boys, boys, boys," Molly would call, and the boys came.

"Thank you," Beth said.

Molly's eyes had been on the dress exclusively; she had not so much as bothered to look high enough to see who was wearing it. If Beth had kept silent she would have been all right. Now Molly glanced at her. "Why, Beth," she said sweetly. "I didn't expect to see *you* at the dance."

Of course not. Beth was the last person a boy would think of asking. Don't ask me where my date is, prayed Beth.

Molly said, "Where's your date? Who'd you come with?"

Beth thought up a good lie, rehearsed it, and accidentally said, "I came alone."

Molly stared at her. "Alone?" she repeated, as if this were a crime. She turned to her date. "Chrissie, darling," she said, "you've got to dance once with Bethie. Just once. Promise me now. It'll make her evening. Promise?"

"Okay," said Christopher. "She can be my good deed for the night." He howled with laughter.

You don't die of humiliation, Beth thought. You suffer over and over.

Molly and Christopher sauntered through the rose arbor, Molly flouncing, Christopher lurching.

Beth followed them quickly, slipping in and over to the side, escaping the photographer's attention.

"You're shaking all over," said Matt. "I guess you got pretty wet after all. Shrug off that coat, because it must be wet through, and get closer to the heater."

She was shivering because of him: his nearness, his presence. But she shrugged off the coat, as he had told her, because now her skin would be bare and she wanted him to touch her.

What would the other kids at the dance think when she and Matt walked in? Would they figure he was some cousin taking pity on her? Or decide Emily had finally blossomed and richly deserved this great guy?

"You know," said Matt, "I'm just driving along here. I don't have any idea where I am or where I'm going. You want me to turn off this road or shall we just cruise all night long?"

She laughed and looked around for landmarks. It was surprisingly hard to figure out where they were. The rain was *thick*. How could rain be thick? "We've gone past the turn we should have taken," she said. "Well, don't turn around. Keep going. We'll take another way. Go past this intersection, and down there, where that truck is, turn left."

"I obey, my lady," said Matt, gently touching her bare shoulder and moving away from her as if it stung. Emily understood. It stung her, too, sending threads of desire through her like a sticky web.

He has to have a girlfriend back home, Emily thought. How could he not have one? Is he taking me to this dance on the sly? Cheating on her? Or is he between girls, and I'm good filler on a dull weekend?

"So one thing I know for sure, Emily," Matt said. "You don't like student government conferences. What *do* you like? I was talking to my mother before I left tonight and she says, 'So what are you two going to talk about?' and

I said, 'Beats me,' and my father said, 'Find out what she's interested in and talk about that.' So give me a list. What are you interested in?"

She giggled. "The world. Truth, beauty, and the meaning of life. Also, baseball, crosswords, and saxophone."

"Emily," said Matt, turning left where she pointed, "I think we have a problem."

"What's that?"

"We have absolutely nothing in common. I do not care about truth, beauty, or the meaning of life; I am interested in ice hockey, cars, and rock music."

"We'll compromise," said Emily. "I'll skip crossword puzzles if you'll skip ice hockey."

He took her left hand in his right. Putting his right hand back on the steering wheel, he drove with her hand like padding. "We'll begin with cars," he said. "I own seven of them."

"*Seven?*"

"I'm restoring them. My father helped me pay for them. I'm learning body work as well as engines. It's a good investment and if we're lucky they'll pay for college. Assuming I go to college. I'd rather do something with cars. Be a mechanic for a racing team."

"Where do you keep all those cars?" said Emily. "You must have an enormous garage."

"Nope. Spread out all over the backyard. The neighbors hate us. My mother isn't too thrilled, either." Matt grinned and squeezed her hand. "But hey, I'm happy."

"Crossword puzzles take up less room," Emily said.

"Yeah, but you have to know how to spell and I —"

The lightning Emily had feared all her life struck.

Their car came around a curve, dipping low, and ahead of them something metallic, something large and indistinguishable blocked the way. Lightning — a huge horrible jagged hot white sheet of it — filled the sky and the car, and its thunder filled her ears and her soul.

Emily screamed.

Matt jammed on the brakes.

They both were flung forward, with no seat belt between them and the dashboard or the windshield.

The sound of tearing metal and crushing rock closed Emily's mind, and her own scream deafened her.

And then there was silence.

Chapter 7

She had taken refuge between a wheelbarrow and a haystack, and two chaperones stood there also. Perhaps they thought it would be a good place to nip mischief in the act. They exclaimed over Beth's dress. It was a temporary sort of conversation; they expected her boyfriend to appear immediately.

Beth Rose could not bear another look of pity. She walked away from them.

Her stomach ceased to churn and knot. It became a solid hard object, like something requiring surgery. *That* would be a way out of this. Ambulance. Perhaps she would require resuscitation. Any emergency room on any Saturday night would be better than this.

Beth Rose faced the dance.

Oh, but Kip had done a wonderful job! The room was romantic beyond imagining. And everyone there dressed so beautifully, paired up so perfectly, smiling so happily.

Beth Rose walked to the fountain. She had no change with her — something, it now occurred to her, that was going to making phoning her mother very difficult. Mentally she chose a silver coin and tossed her wish into the fountain. The band began playing a hot wild piece that everybody knew; it had been number two or three for weeks now, struggling for first place. Beth ached to dance to it. A fast dance in Aunt Madge's dress. She couldn't picture it. But, oh, to try!

In the shadows on the far side of the fountain stood a boy. Dark in his formal suit, he was like a shadow himself. Beth Rose dreamed on him, and when he detached himself from the shadows, and walked toward her, it seemed like part of the dream.

It was Gary Anthony. Beth could only smile at herself. If there was ever a boy on whom she could have a crush, it would be Gary. She didn't allow herself crushes. They hurt too much, for nothing ever came of them. The boy never noticed her, let alone returned her feelings.

Gary was a senior for whom school was a necessary evil, and for him graduation would be a great relief. Undoubtedly he would enter his father's thriving restaurant business. Beth loved eating there on the off chance she might see Gary. For he was remarkably handsome.

A lot of boys became handsome once you got to know them, because their personalities were intertwined with their features, and you could no longer tell, once you liked them, where one began and the other left off. But Gary was handsome by anybody's definition. His hair was dark and extremely curly; he had dark eyes, fair skin, and a surprisingly sweet smile. She couldn't remember hearing Gary laugh. He simply smiled, or for an especially funny occasion, grinned. She knew girls who practiced funny stories to tell Gary, just to get that grin.

He wasn't tall, but because he was on track and wrestling teams he was much more muscular than most boys his age. She had never seen him dressed up before. She thought of him exclusively in old jeans, a soft old shirt, and one of two pullover sweaters — an ivory fisherman's knit, and a navy cotton crew. How absurd, thought Beth Rose. I know his entire wardrobe.

Gary walked toward her.

She watched him as if they were on film. When he spoke she was astonished. She had forgotten he was real. "Beth Rose?" he said questioningly.

"Hello, Gary," she said.

They stared at each other. His soft dark eyes moved very slowly down the dress, looking at the lace, the softly falling folds of pale pale pink, the tips of slippers showing beneath the hem. He looked at her hair, and her earrings, and then into her eyes. He said, "You look wonderful. Absolutely wonderful."

She could neither move nor think. She simply smiled at him; his smile — sweet, but revealing nothing.

He said, "Are you waiting for somebody, Beth Rose?"

She had never thought her two names went well together. The names took too long to say; they were awkward; most people were reluctant to bother. When she was little, the other little kids shortened it to Brose. Now they didn't bother; they said Beth — if they said anything at all.

For the first time in her life, Beth Rose Chapman flirted. "I'm waiting for you," she said.

They stood very still.

The band played so fiercely she thought the light fixtures might explode under the pressure of the sound.

Couples entered the dance behind Beth, split like rivers over rocks in the water to get past them, and circled the fountain.

Gary said softly, "My good luck."

He curled his fingers around hers, moved so gracefully to her side it was like an old-fashioned dance step, and began walking her toward the fountain. From his pocket he drew pennies, and handed her one.

"Make a wish." It was a command.

I wanted this to happen so much that I'm fantasizing right during the dance, Beth Rose thought. Actually, Gary isn't standing here and I don't have a penny in my hand. People are calling the ambulance for me, but not because of the knot in my stomach. They're going to lock me in a padded room.

Gary's hand, with the penny, stayed in hers. His hand was warm and rough and not as large as she would have expected. Her own hand was much slimmer, much paler, but their fingers were the same length. Her nails, painted deep rose, reflected in his palm. She tossed the penny.

I wish for Gary all night long.

The penny fell into the shallows. It lay among the other pennies, and after she blinked, she could no longer tell which penny it was.

In a normal voice, Gary said, "I'm starving. Are you? Let's see what Kip planned for food, huh? My dad catered some of it, but I eat that stuff all the time. Let's see what else there is."

Gary Anthony. Talking to her as if she really were his date.

Beth Rose glided down the scarlet path with him, her dress rustling against his legs, her hand still in his.

Molly looked up from Christopher, with whom she seemed to be having trouble, and her jaw fell. Sue and her date, Page and her date, Caitlin and her date — they all stared. Each girl turned to the others and Beth fancied she could read their lips. Is that Beth Rose? With Gary?

Anne Stephens and Con Winters, locked together as always, glanced up. Beth Rose read identical confusion on them. They could not quite identify her. Well, there were some seven hundred juniors and the same number of seniors; it was not surprising. But it still hurt. She had admired Anne for so many years; she would have liked to think Anne could recognize her face, at least.

Gary was good friends with Con. He stopped to talk. Anne smiled the blank smile of someone waiting to be introduced. "This," said Gary, smiling into Beth's eyes and not theirs, "is Beth Rose Chapman."

Beth felt as if her name had just been entered

on some sort of social honor roll. Con shook her hand. Anne smiled more naturally. "You are wearing the most beautiful dress, Beth," said Anne. "I've never seen one like it. Is it an antique?"

"Yes. My great aunt Madge wore it to her prom fifty years ago."

Anne clapped her hands, laughing. "I love it! What a wonderful family tradition! I hope when I have a family —"

Her voice broke off abruptly. She bit her lip, and stared off into the decorations. Neither boy noticed. They were talking about food. Con was recommending the little round hot things with the sausage. "Yeah," said Gary, "my father made those. They're always good."

"Are you all right?" said Beth to Anne.

Anne stared at her with a queerly frozen look.

"We're going to sit down over here," said Con, pointing to a pair of oak park benches Kip had gotten donated for the evening. "Come sit with us after you get some food."

"I'm fine," said Anne quietly, just to Beth, and Beth had the strangest sensation of having been given some sort of message.

"Here's your plate," said Gary, handing her a small paper one with a Thanksgiving-type design of turkeys and cornucopias and a dark orange napkin. She glanced back at Anne, but Anne's back was to her now. It must have been the light, thought Beth. This is my night to fall into fantasies that mean nothing.

"Thank you," she said to Gary. What is Gary

thinking? she wondered. Is he trying to figure out why I'm here alone? What is he planning for his evening? Why did he come alone — he of all people? Am I, Beth Rose Chapman, really going to sit out the dance with Anne Stephens, Con Winter, and Gary Anthony?

Gary took her arm — she who had never had a boy escort her anywhere, ever — and they walked back to where Con and Anne were sitting. It took real juggling on Gary's part to manage his plate, his drink, and her arm. All that waitering at his father's restaurant, she thought, but she didn't kid him; she had no idea what Gary would consider amusing.

Anne was grateful for the food. If she couldn't hang onto Con, at least she could hang onto a plate and a plastic cup of cider. She watched her fingers, and the fingers seemed very calm considering the position their owner was in. I'm falling apart, thought Anne. It's going to hit me right now, right here, in public.

She looked at Con, and he looked away instantly, saying, "Here comes Gary. Doesn't Beth look fantastic?"

"Lovely," said Anne mechanically.

Where do you stand, Con? she thought. With me . . . or away from me?

She felt no particular need to return Gary's smile. Gary was an unusual person, Anne had always thought. He drifted. Friendly, yes, to everybody; she thought if she were to mention any name at all, Gary would say, "Oh, he's a friend of mine" and mean it. But nobody attached themselves to Gary; not male friends, not girlfriends. Gary kept more distance between himself and other people than anyone she had ever known. And yet he was totally likable.

Maybe he's wiser than I, thought Anne. If I had kept a little more distance between Con and me . . . .

She stared at Beth Rose. Beth had a transparent otherworldly aura, as if she had stepped out of some other existence to join them. Where did you come from? thought Anne giddily. Let me go there, too. Maybe it's safe.

The boys talked college football.

Their words were so much babble to her.

Babble. Babies babbled. What would a real-life baby be like? Instead of senior year. Instead of a life of her own. This other little person's life. A person who would be around for eighteen years. *I'm* not even eighteen yet, thought Anne. I'm seventeen. I'll have to take care of this person longer than I've even been alive.

Chapter 8

When Kip and Roddy arrived at Westerly High, the doorman opened the passenger side to escort the girl in while the boy parked the car and got soaked running back. Sopping wet, but still impressive in his uniform, the doorman was surprised to find Roddy when he whipped open the door. He looked at Kip, whose long gown was still pulled back over her knees so it wouldn't tangle when she shifted. "Perhaps your passenger could park the car for you, miss," he suggested, "and I'll walk you indoors."

Kip thought, Well, I certainly hired the right man here. She started to get out. Roddy said weakly, "Except that I can't drive a car with manual transmission, Kip. Both our cars have automatic." He gave her a pitiful smile. "Otherwise I'd be glad to."

Too stupid even to drive a real car! thought Kip, loathing him. She, who was usually the first to sympathize, the first to offer comfort, ignored the misery on Roddy's face. Tonight she felt she could safely hold him responsible for all her own woes. "That's all right, Roddy," she said rather nastily. "I'll get soaked walking back and we'll be a matched pair."

Naturally the only parking place left had puddles on both sides. Kip stepped out into two inches of cold water, ruining her satin slippers. She was so disgusted she almost didn't bother to lift her long skirt, either, but at the last second conceded she didn't want to ruin it, too, so they ran together through the puddles, Kip holding her skirts very high.

But once inside, her spirits lifted slightly. They'd run into two other couples, who entered the parking lot by the back and had not known there was a doorman in front, so all four of them were soaked, too. Laughing the way people do when they share a misfortune, the girls fixed each other's hair, commented sadly on the state of their shoes, and the boys wiped themselves down as if they'd come from showers, and rolled their eyes at each other.

And nothing could have been more wonderful than walking into what only that morning had been a mere school cafeteria.

Every inch of it was Kip's — and every inch was perfect. Kip got tears in her eyes looking. The band was playing, the decorations were perfect, and perfectly lighted, the food was being gobbled, and everybody looked happy and beautiful.

"Kip!" exclaimed Roddy. "You did a grand job."

Yeah, she thought. Too bad I couldn't arrive with somebody grand as well.

They followed the scarlet runner she had installed just that afternoon. Every single couple they passed broke away from whatever they were doing to compliment her on the fantastic job she'd done.

"Oh, Kip!" came the cries. "Wonderful! I'm having such a good time!"

"Kip! It looks so terrific. You did such a good job!"

"Kip! If you hadn't agreed to chair this dance, the administration wouldn't have let us have it again this year. It's because of *you* we have this at all!"

Kip bloomed.

She no longer felt wet and scraggly and worthless. She didn't even feel angry at Roddy for being alive. She felt proud and happy, and when she glanced his way, he was smiling timidly at her, as if they really had something in common and had come together as willing dates, not a pair of last minute losers.

Anne Stephens kissed Kip on both cheeks. Anne did things like that. She always seemed so much more secure and sophisticated than anybody else. Kip felt it was having Con around that did it. With a person like that at your side, week in and week out, you could cope with anything. "Lovely work, Kip," said Anne, in her mellow voice.

Kip loved Anne's speaking voice, "I know I've told you a hundred times, Anne, but you have to go into radio or television with that voice and your looks."

To Kip's surprise, Anne didn't answer. She

looked oddly bitter and frantic and she simply walked off.

"That was odd," Kip said to Roddy. Roddy said, "What was odd?" and Kip realized Roddy had seen nothing amiss; in fact he was looking after Anne dreamily, as one half in love. Oh, you *fink!* thought Kip. Even *you* have to dream of somebody better!

"Let's get something to eat," Roddy suggested.

Kip was always ready to eat, and anyhow, since she'd ordered all that food, she needed to check out the quality. They walked toward the barnboard shed, where junior high boys were lugging in more cases of soda, and bringing hot trays in from the kitchen — and there stood Molly Nelmes and Christopher Vann.

Kip had never liked Molly. Molly didn't buy candy bars when the school band was raising money for new uniforms; Molly wouldn't take an hour to sell school pins when the basketball team was raising money for summer basketball camp scholarships; Molly wouldn't sign the petition to get the student parking lot resurfaced. She wouldn't even raise her hand to vote during student government meetings because she skipped them and went shopping instead. Molly never got in trouble, either, because the principal was a typical male who responded to her charms just like all the other boys.

As for Christopher, Kip had worked with him when she was a sophomore and he a senior. Christopher had a lot going for him, but he had a real tendency to take credit for the work being done by his committee. In Kip's opinion, when Christopher applied to college, half his application was lies. He hadn't done much; he'd just been there and taken credit for it. But how was a college to know? Even most of the kids didn't, because Christopher was such a glad-hand politician they thought he was working, too. Only the really hard workers like Kip knew he was half real, half cheat.

And tonight . . . wholly drunk.

For a moment Kip was scared. Could he have gotten drunk *here?* If there was so much as a whiff of liquor at this school there would never be another dance as long as she lived.

If those two slobs sneaked booze into my dance, I'll kill them, she thought. She had a quick sip from each punch bowl, but no. One was a ginger ale and sherbet mix, the other spiced apple cider. Almost everybody was having soda, though.

The first thing Kip said to them was, "So, Christopher, what are you doing home from Harvard?"

"Slumming," said Christopher promptly.

Molly laughed.

Kip flushed. Her dance was a slum compared to a Harvard dance — was that what he meant? Now when she looked at her beautiful decorations, they seemed very amateurish and spotty, and they embarrassed her.

To Roddy, Christopher said, "Who are you, kid? You look sorta familiar."

Next to Christopher, Roddy did look like a kid — scrawny and unformed. However, Christopher was getting heavier. Kip debated saying so out loud and decided against it.

"This," said Molly in a lazy drawl, "is my little Roddy. When I don't have anything else to do, I go out with him. Remember? He was hanging around me at the Pou-Belle?"

This was so clearly true, by the way Roddy flushed and hung his head, that Kip wanted to smack them both. Why did Roddy cringe like that? Why didn't he stand up to Molly? He should laugh at her, or shrug, not dwindle into a puddle.

Christopher laughed, loudly and drunkenly. "He's really the bottom of the barrel, Molly. Thought you could do better. Look, there's even a barrel over here. We could toss out all those stupid apples and stuff old Roddy in and see if he falls to the bottom."

"He will," said Molly with conviction.

Roddy wilted even more. It made Kip furious that she had to be the one who talked back to Molly. "You don't exactly rise like cream to the top, yourself, you know, Molly," said Kip sharply. "In fact, if I had to define where *you* stand, I'd say that — "

"Let it go, Kip," said Roddy, touching her arm. Not taking it, no — nothing so forceful.

"You're going to let her talk about you like that?" demanded Kip.

"Just drop it, okay?" mumbled Roddy. "People are looking at us."

"At *us*, maybe," said Christopher. "*You* they don't even see, Roddy."

In a last desperate effort to remove himself, Roddy said, "Let's dance, Kip."

The last thing she wanted to do was dance. She wanted to throw Molly and Christopher out. She glared at Roddy, and now he cringed from *her*. Kip turned her back on Roddy. Her skirt swirled noisily, adding a flourish of sound effects to her gesture. She stalked away from all of them.

"Great dance, Kip," said a voice.

She managed a smile, and looked up, trying to keep her anger at Roddy, Molly, and Christopher off her face.

It was Gary.

Only the handsomest boy she'd ever had a crush on. A flush of delight came to Kip's cheeks. Gary had an elusive style. Nobody quite knew where he stood, only that it would be nice to stand there with him. Kip's heart raced. "Thank you," she said, thinking, *we* could dance. Oh, Gary, ask *me* to dance!

His arm circled another girl.

It was — Kip stared in disbelief — it was Beth Rose Chapman.

She almost said out loud, "I don't believe it. You asked *her*?" She choked back the words. The flush on her face deepened, for fear Gary had understood.

"I love your dress, Kip," said Beth Rose softly.

She had to look down to remember what her dress looked like. The top was very plain, but also very low cut. When she looked down it was like announcing that Gary should look there, too. She was doubly humiliated. But I do look good in it, she thought. She waited, hoping Gary would also tell her the dress was nice.

He said, "Did you lose Roddy? He's over by the band, probably looking for you."

He was smiling at her. He didn't seem to intend irony.

Kip was back at her original low. I get my first date and it's with pathetic Roddy, because Molly had a better offer. I run into Gary Anthony and it's his date who says I look nice. Beth Rose. She's as pathetic as Roddy. If I had to bracket any two losers it would be them.

Gary said to Beth, "Let's dance again." Beth Rose beamed at him. She really was very lovely, in an unreal sort of way. It was the dress: dated, unusual, a dress that somehow transformed Beth into somebody special. *But I have a lovely dress, too!* Kip wanted to scream.

Gary escorted Beth Rose down Kip's scarlet carpet, onto the dance floor Kip had set up, and it was Beth's face he smiled down upon and Beth's waist his hand touched.

Why am I kidding myself? she thought. I'm no winner. I'm a loser. Even wretched nasty Molly is more a winner than I am. Christopher may be drunk, and college may have turned him nasty and insulting, but he's one heck of a date and it isn't me he flew back to Westerly for.

She turned to dance with Roddy, because she had to do something with another person: She could stand alone not another moment. But

Roddy was not where Gary had said. He was gone.

The rock music she ordinarily loved gave her a matching rhythmic headache. I hurt Roddy because he was there, she thought.

People were staring at her. Poor Kip, she could hear them thinking. Alone at her own dance.

"Please be all right!" he was crying. "Oh, God! Oh, Emily! Please! Be all right. It wasn't us that crashed. It was just a tree coming down. We aren't even hit, we're just blocked." Matt's hands circled her and pulled her back against him. "I should never have taken this car. No seatbelts. It's all my fault. Emily, talk to me."

Emily thought dizzily, this is dialogue out of a sinking ocean liner movie. "I'm okay," she said. "I didn't actually pass out, I just sort of lost my breath."

His hands swept over her forehead and face, exploring in the dark, feeling for blood or broken bones. She could feel his panic when his chest lurched with breathing hard. "It's okay," she said to him, "we're both okay."

For a moment they held each other limply. They were neither dead nor bleeding. Little else mattered.

A horrid weird crackle startled them both.

Emily swallowed in fright. Lying on the large flat hood of the old car was a live wire, sparkling like a firecracker on the Fourth of July.

"Don't move," whispered Matt hoarsely.

Whispering back, as if the wire was listening, Emily said, "Why not?"

"Because whatever we're touching right now isn't conducting electricity. If we shift position, we might come into contact with the current."

"Now there's a comforting thought," said Emily, but actually she was comforted. There were worse things than lying in Matt's arms. And Westerly had excellent volunteer response from both fire department and ambulance. They'd be here momentarily. Or the utility company, as soon as the houses around reported an electricity outage. She and Matt would be freed, and their date would be an adventure story to tell for years.

Even the knowledge that there were virtually no houses on this back road, and there might be nobody to report the wires down didn't bother Emily. She would be perfectly content to repose against Matt for hours. Although her feet were already getting cold.

The Ford's headlights gleamed through the branches of the downed pine tree. "At least your grandfather won't kill you," Emily said to Matt. "You slammed on the brakes when you heard the tree coming down and saved the car as well as us."

Matt's fingers tightened on her wrist. "Oh, my God," he whispered. "Emily, it wasn't the tree coming down I heard. There was another car. Look through the branches. The car over there is totaled."

She sat up slightly.

A large branch had stabbed through the driver's window of the wrecked car. Glass glistened like smashed ice. If there were people in the car, they were not moving.

When Matt spoke, Emily could feel his fear: His lips were numb and the words were stiff. "They could be bleeding to death in there," he mumbled. "I have to help."

"We can't move!" Emily said fiercely, grabbing him. "We can't get out of the car. We'll be electrocuted."

For another half minute they remained frozen. She watched the tiny white numbers flashing on her digital watch, flicking seconds in her face. Seconds in which people could die.

"We can't be cowards," said Matt. He attempted a smile. "What's a live wire between friends?"

I am a coward, she thought. I admit it. I don't want to touch a live wire, or a car with a live wire lying on it. I don't want to crawl around in the dark over broken glass and —

"There might not be another car for quite a while," said Matt. "If we don't help, nobody will."

Emily shuddered convulsively.

Matt reached for his own door.

"No!" she cried. "You can't get out that side. The wire is right there. You have to get out my side." Which meant she would have to get out first.

Lightning ripped through the sky, plunging them into savage light, and then vanished. Thunder came instantly, and the old Ford shivered with the boom. Emily sobbed, but Matt didn't hear her over the thunder.

Shifting slowly to her right, each micro-second waiting for the blast of electricity that would burn through her heart, Emily thought, Am I doing this because somebody needs our help? Or am I doing it to impress Matt? So he'll like me still?

What good will a date do if I'm going to be buried?

With utter terror, Emily put her bare hand on the metal of the door handle.

Nobody in the cafeteria saw the lightning or heard the thunder. The band was giving nature excellent competition.

Anne didn't even hear the band.

She thought only of Con.

Con's family moved a great deal. His mother loved to restore houses. She was always finding a "treasure" (which Con referred to as "the newest dump") and restoring it. When the new kitchen gleamed, the wallpaper was all up, the last electrician and mason had gone, she lost interest in the house, sold it for a profit, and moved on. Mr. Winter never cared. He was an athlete, whose life rotated around the games he coached, the games he played in, and the games he watched on television.

Con was their only child.

His mother made a point of finishing his bedroom first, so that in the midst of dust and turmoil he could shut the door and be reasonably civilized. But there were three high schools in the city and Con had attended two of them;

eleven junior highs and Con had gone to three of those.

She'd met Con during a transfer. He walked into Anne's seventh grade social studies class on a bright March morning when the wind whipped hard enough to make even seventh graders dream of kites. He sat next to Anne. They never spoke. Once Con rode home with Anne during a snowstorm, when Con's mother didn't come to pick him up. It would not have crossed Mrs. Winter's mind to worry over how Con would get home; he had been self-sufficient since he was ten.

"How do you like school, Con?" said Mrs. Winters.

"Fine," said Con.

In April they moved again, so Con was at another junior high. Anne saw him once at the shopping center, and another time she walked into the pet store and he was buying food for rats he kept for a biology class experiment. They talked briefly of white rats.

In ninth grade, Con walked into Anne's class again. Only this time it was French, and Con startled all of them by speaking it fluently. He'd spent the summer in France at an American camp. Anne fell in love with him in about ten minutes.

Maybe it was eight minutes.

He'd grown earlier than most boys. Still thin, with no muscles yet, he was five nine when most ninth grade boys were still five four. *"Bonjour, Mademoiselle,"* he said to Anne in a scratchy sexy voice. *"Je t'aime."*

The class laughed. They needed a clown. French was boring, boring, boring. But Con turned out not to be a clown. He had seen Anne, sat next to her, and said, and meant it, *"Je t'aime."*

Mrs. Stephens wouldn't let them date. "You're much too young," she scolded. But she let Con come over all the time and soon he was a fixture in the Stephens household. Two or three times a week he'd have dinner with them, visit their cousins with them, go to the movies with them, mow the lawn for them. And Anne went with Con's mother to look at wallpaper and watched Sunday afternoon sports programs with Con's father.

They talked continually. School, their plans, their friends, their hopes and dreams. Until they discovered sex. Then, somehow, there was much less talk. Even though it seemed to Anne there was so much more to talk about, Con talked less. The more they shared physically, the less she knew of Con himself.

The deception involved sickened her.

Always the pretending, always the lying, to one set of parents or the other, and often to themselves. Hiding from family. Getting up afterward and running home as if nothing had happened. Con would never talk about that, either. When it bothered her the most, Con was nothing but a shrug, a silent person waiting for her to get out of the car.

And yet she loved him so much!

What happens when I go home and tell them? thought Anne. After they stop screaming, after they stop weeping, the questions begin.

But Anne, when did you. . . .

You know how I said we were going to the movies? We went over to Con's old house, and lay on the football blanket you keep in the trunk of our car, and used the upstairs bedroom.

But Anne, you told us. . . .

I lied.

But Anne, we had faith in you.

You were dumb.

Con, who rarely read books, once showed her a book jacket. "Here," he said. "Read this."

Anne read. The author was twenty-nine. Since leaving home (at a tender age, it said) he had been a logger in Alaska, a bartender in Santa Fe, a navy signalman in the Pacific, an instructor of motor repair in Africa, a free-lance reporter in Afghanistan, and raced yachts off the coast of England. He'd had pet jaguars (animals, not cars) and his hobby was refinishing antique fire engines.

"He made that all up," said Anne. "Probably lives in Detroit and works in an automobile factory."

Con was furious at this remark. "That's my life, Anne. I made a copy of this in the Xerox machine so I'd always have it around. That's what I'm going to do."

Anne laughed. "Don't be silly," she said, hugging him. "You'd miss me too much."

Con just smiled.

Now she remembered that smile. An I-know-more-than-you-do smile. He's always loved me, she thought. He'll go right on loving me. But he won't stay. A baby? Be real! Con has no ties. He's used to moving. He won't think a minute before picking up and going on to the next adventure. He'll be off for the Far East and I'll be at home with a wailing baby in wet diapers.

Gary was busy talking to Beth Rose.

Con was looking around for somebody — anybody — so he wouldn't have to talk to Anne.

She said, "Con. Con, please. We've got to — "

"Don't start anything," he said. His voice was almost inaudible, but ferocious, as if he could kill her. When she looked into his eyes she saw nothing there but rage. For one terrible moment she was physically afraid of Con. Con, whom she loved.

Con turned to Gary and Beth Rose, because they were there. "Don't you have a nickname, Beth Rose? I don't remember calling you by such a long pretty name."

Beth Rose could not remember Con calling her anything, ever. "Well, sometimes people call me Brose. It's shorter."

"But do you like it?" said Con. "It sounds masculine, and you are the most fragile, feminine thing at this dance."

Anne heard that. He is talking to me, she thought. He's talking to me through Beth. He's saying, Annie, old girl, this is *your* problem. I can flirt with anybody I please, and you can't stop me.

Gary looked faintly puzzled, and his eyes rested on Anne, trying to figure this one out. He couldn't, so he did what boys always did: He moved on. "Let's dance again," he said to Beth, and didn't wait for an answer, but spun her out into the dancing couples and vanished into the press of long gowns.

Con never looked at her. He turned and yelled, "Christopher Vann! So how's the Ivy League, buddy? Hey, Molly. Looking good, lady. You tried this punch yet? It's weird. Green sherbet floating around in it like frogs hatching."

Molly laughed hysterically. Christopher whapped Con on the shoulder. Anne said, "I'm going to fix my hair. I'll be right back."

She could not seem to cross the cafeteria. Everybody she had ever known blocked her passage. How lovely you are, Anne, they said to her. How nice the dance is, Anne, they said to her. How's Con, Anne? Time for him to move on again, isn't it? They laughed.

It seemed to her generations had passed, and eons scraped by, in the time it took to get out, to reach the girls' room, to be safely alone.

It was very clean. Much cleaner than usual. No doubt Kip had arranged that, too. Kip was remarkable.

If I cry, my eyes will be red and my makeup will run. I'll look so awful I won't ever be able to leave the bathroom.

But I have to cry. It's like a volcano in me, bursting through my faults. I'm going to cry buckets and there's nothing I can do.

She walked into the last stall, carefully shot the bolt behind herself, and leaned against the gray graffiti-scratched metal.

Chapter 9

"The wind just blew the wire off my car," said Matt. "We're all right. Come on, hurry up, open the door."

A gust of vicious wind flicked sharp cold rain into Emily's face. She had never seen Nature so wild. There had been no forecast for this sort of storm. Rain, high winds, a little bit of lightning — that's what the television said. A lot they knew.

And now that the wire was blown off the car, where was it? Emily wanted to know. Lying beneath her feet?

Matt climbed over her to get out. She didn't even care that his muddy shoes left tracks on her formal dress. "Get the flashlight out of the backseat," he said to her. Glad to stay in the car, Emily flipped over the seat, found the flashlight, and handed it to him.

Matt vanished.

There was no lightning to illuminate him. He did not stand in the light from the Ford headlights. The other car's front end had been completely bashed in and had no lights. He had been swallowed by the night. She shrieked his name. "Matt! Are you all right!"

But the wind was louder than her cries.

Emily could feel the lightning hitting her. She could feel what it would be like to be cooked from the inside: having that electricity course through her body, ripping through her limbs, cooking her brain. What would be left of me after lightning got me? thought Emily. Would I still have a soul after my mind was literally fried?

Above her the huge trees tossed wildly, their branches rubbing together with a scream like wolves after prey.

Very slowly Emily Edmundson pushed herself across the leather seat, onto the wet cold parts the wind had drenched. Very slowly she levered herself outside the car entirely and stood on the pavement, while prickly evergreen needles stabbed through her gown and rain wet her hair down to her skull.

If I step on that live wire, she thought, will there be time to know what's happening? Time to mutter, Oh for heaven's sake, in disgust before I die?

She climbed over branches. Her gown caught on the sticky sap, and the sharp prongs of a branch ripped it. She gathered the dress neatly around her waist, fought grimly through the tree, and reached the side of the wrecked car ... a collection of rips, tears, and mud.

Matt was halfway in the front seat. The driver's door was bent so he couldn't open it all the way. It kept slapping against him when the wind caught it. His ribs will be broken while he stands there, Emily thought.

"He's bleeding bad," said Matt when she slid over next to him. "Unconscious. I can keep enough pressure on this major wound to stop most of the bleeding, though. But Emily, you've got to go for an ambulance. There was a house up the road half a mile."

Half a mile? In this? Alone?

Matt's position was awful: He was hunched in a backbreaking way over the victim. Rainwater ran off a tree branch and into his hair; the wind smacked the car door against him again. When Emily did not move, he frowned at her. "Hurry up!" he yelled over the wind, and went back to the hurt man behind the wheel.

She climbed back over the fallen fir tree. She was afraid of the woods. She didn't dare circle through the forest and come back out on the road again. Lightning thoughtfully struck again, so she could see where she was going. The road, in her one terrified glance, appeared to be free of wires.

But the wire was there somewhere.

Waiting for her.

Emily began walking forward. She tiptoed, so that less of her foot could come in contact with something. Twenty steps forward she touched something with her left foot. Emily screamed, louder than she or anybody else in history had ever screamed before. The scream itself was so terrifying that it made Emily leap forward, moved by her own adrenalin. It felt like an electric shock, and even as she ran she sobbed, thinking, *It got me, it got me.*

She had no dress left to speak of. One huge portion of the skirt had torn entirely away, and the rest dragged after her like a broken leg.

And to think that none of this would have happened if she had paid attention and told Matt to take the turn he was supposed to take.

Only hours before she had had the pampering of her life. That hot perfumed beauty shop. Sitting under the hooded dryer, dreamily staring through an old *Glamour*. The babble of voices around her was drowned out by the hot air that rushed to bake her new curls. And when Emily came out, there was the wonderful warm brushing of her hair. Nothing was more pleasurable than having her hair brushed. But then, she thought, waiting for Michael the hairdresser to finish her, her sensual experiences were zero. From what she had read, there were many things more wonderful than having your hair brushed. As Michael used a blow dryer to finish one little curl, then frowned into the mirror and tried an electric curling iron to perfect the lock, Emily pretended that tonight, at the Autumn Leaves Dance, she would find out about some of those wonderful things.

Now what could she look like?

Emily hated going swimming, because when she came out of the water with her hair plastered to her skull and her makeup gone or staining her cheeks, she looked ridiculous if not downright ugly.

And here she was utterly destroyed by wind and water.

And oh, so cold. The temperature felt like February in a blizzard. She ran, her side hurting. I'll probably die of exposure, she thought. She slipped on a patch of leaves slick from rain and fell heavily on her side. She wasn't hurt, but the heel had broken off her right shoe. She tripped immediately, fell, and tore her knee open.

Thunder.

It rattled her heart, so close it was like being inside the bass drums of the marching band. Emily felt as if she had been staggering forever through the wind, attacked by lightning, assaulted by the branches that lay in the road like so many animal traps in the dark.

Another tree began to fall.

Emily froze in place, terrified. The tree fell with remarkable, *Twilight Zone*-like slowness. It took her a while to realize that its own roots and other tree branches were slowing it down. It came to rest rather quietly on the far side of the road. Emily could not even hear the sobs that were wracking her over the howling of the wind.

She could not believe this was Westerly, only a mile or two from her own home. This was some other, terrible planet.

Ahead of her she saw the lights of the only house on the road.

How could they not have lost their electricity?

Was she truly in the *Twilight Zone*?

Or maybe it had been the cable tv wire, or the

telephone wire, that had terrified her so thoroughly.

She stumbled forward.

I can never go to the dance now, she thought. It's all ruined. My hair, my dress, my lace stockings, my shoes.

She pounded on the door, and fell inside, weeping, as it was opened to her.

Slow music.

Sweetly, softly, wafting them all the more deeply into each other's arms. Beth Rose vaguely recognized the melody. It's usually much faster, she thought. The band changed it so we could dance slow.

Me. Dancing in Gary's arms. Slow.

She truly felt like Cinderella in Prince Charming's arms. Aunt Madge will like that, she thought. Aunt Madge as Fairy Godmother. It's perfect.

She found herself glancing at her tiny watch, to see how many hours till midnight, and the end of the magic spell.

They had dimmed the lights and turned off the wild, flashing strobe lights that had accompanied the fast music. The band played under enough light for them to recognize each other's faces, but certainly not to read music by. The kids danced almost in darkness. Beth loved it. "If the storm knocks out the electricity, we'll never even know," she said to Gary.

He laughed. "We won't hear from the guitars again any time soon, if the electricity goes." He put both arms around her now. She had never danced close with a boy. It was too much for concentration. She could not maneuver her feet when Gary's face was against hers like that; she couldn't think. But Gary did nothing except sway slightly, and shift a few inches when another couple touched them. That she could manage.

The fabric of her gown rustled against his jacket. The lace that covered her bosom was crushed against the starched front of his evening shirt. Her bare skin touched the white cloth. For a moment she was too tense to relax. He touched her hair and she let herself lean on his shoulder. He was, she guessed, three or four inches taller than she. It was perfect. She could lean on him comfortably, move her own weight in rhythm with him, and resting on his shoulder was like falling in love.

She closed her eyes. It was wonderful that way, because nothing intruded on her happy thoughts. When at last she opened her eyes, it was even nicer. She was used to the dark, and she could now see that people were looking at her.

She knew that she was as beautiful as Gary was handsome. She knew that they made a perfect couple. The people who did not know her wanted to; and the people who *did* know her were intrigued.

She wanted to shout to them all — it's me! I've joined! I'm not the outsider anymore. I can do all the things you guys can do. I can win the games, run the races, have the boys. Just look!

She found herself almost laughing with delight.

"What's so funny, Beth?" said Gary. He drew back from her so he could see her face. She beamed at him, happiness as much a part of her as her eyebrows and skin. "I'm just having such a good time," she said joyously. "I didn't know I would have such a good time! Thank you, Gary."

To her surprise and shock, Gary's face became expressionless.

He did not, as she had hoped, lean down to kiss her.

He looked away.

I did something wrong, Beth Rose thought. What could I have done wrong? I was just being honest. I thought you were supposed to be honest.

The dance ended.

They stood without speaking on the dance floor and couples all around them hugged and went back to their seats, or headed over for refreshments.

Gary gave her a perfunctory smile, and she knew in an instant he was going to leave her.

Panic walked over her like an insect, and she shivered. Gary looked faintly puzzled, but nothing more.

But the music started up again, this time fast and rowdy and wild, and everyone left on the dance floor began shouting along with the song, and stomping their feet. Gary danced. He was really dancing alone, not even touching or looking at her, but she danced, too. The dance was wrong for the dress. It was a dance for blue jeans and a torn sweat shirt. Here she was in a froth of pale pink and antique ivory. But she danced anyhow, lifting the skirt so she wouldn't catch her feet on the hems of lace. It was weird to dance with her hands holding onto the dress. Beth liked to use her hands and arms a lot when she danced to rock, and now they weren't available. What could she look like?

Whatever she looked like, Gary seemed to be pleased. He circled her, came back to her, grinned at her, and danced like a madman.

I know what I did wrong, Beth Rose thought. I made him responsible for giving me a good time.

I've got to remember he didn't bring me here. He just materialized at the door when I did. I cannot place demands on him, or expect anything from him. I've got to leave every door open just the way it was, so he can leave any time without feeling guilty. He's going to leave anyhow; I have to let him leave easily.

The joy faded from the wild dance.

What an assignment! Have fun — but know it will end any moment.

Truly, thought Beth Rose Chapman, I am Cinderella. But there is no glass slipper. He won't come to my house tomorrow, begging to marry me. I have this minute, and that is all.

Their name was Gorman. They were her parents' age, and they were very calm, very reassuring, and their telephone worked. After they reached the ambulance and the utility company, they called Mr. Edmundson to bring Emily a change of clothing. She sat, wrapped in an old afghan, on a kitchen chair, feeling that she could sleep for a week.

"Do you think I could take a shower?" she said. Her voice sounded floaty to her, removed from herself, somehow.

"In a little bit, dear," said Mrs. Gorman gently. "I think we're going to send you to the emergency room first, though."

"Me?" said Emily. "The lightning missed me and so did the tree."

"The gravel didn't," said Mr. Gorman.

Emily could remember no gravel.

"Honey, your shoes fell apart," said Mrs. Gorman, "and stockings aren't much protection against a gravel road."

"Amazing you could run on it at all," said her husband.

Emily looked at her feet, and quickly looked away. She did not care for the sight of blood.

I was so afraid of the lightning and the dark and the thunder and Matt's disapproval that I didn't think of being afraid of other things, too. Except my clothes. I didn't want to ruin them.

The Gormans hovered over her, telling her how wonderful she was to have suffered so much to rescue a stranger in distress.

Emily said nothing. She was ashamed to admit she suffered only so Matt would not think less of her, and ran not so much to save a life as to get out of the storm.

The afghan she was wrapped in was very old. Any itchiness from the yarn was long gone; there was nothing left of it but softness and weight and comfort. She felt herself falling asleep. The whole school is dancing, she thought, and I'm sleeping it off in somebody's living room while we wait for an ambulance.

She was aware of sirens, and flashing lights, and the Gormans talking, but nothing seemed related to Emily. She was surprised to be put on a stretcher. "Doesn't mean there's anything seriously wrong with you, honey," said the attendant, grinning at her. "It's just the way we do it. Lie down, kid. You're quite the heroine. You know who that guy was in the car? Your boyfriend saved his life."

My boyfriend, thought Emily, savoring those two words, smiling at such a lovely thought. "Who?" she said, as they strapped her in.

"Jasper L. Chase."

She had never heard of him. "He wasn't that badly hurt then?" she said anxiously.

"He was hurt real bad. Your boyfriend saved his life," he repeated. "And so did you, getting here. You can be real proud, honey."

"How come you're not dressed in white?" she asked. They slid her into the ambulance and closed the doors behind them.

"We're volunteers. We have twelve-hour shifts of being on call," he explained. "I was at home working on my son's train set. That's why I'm a little greasy around the edges."

"I've never minded a little grease around the edges," Emily said.

"Good thing, sweetheart, because if there's one thing you need, it's a long hot shower."

He was joking, but that remark took all the fun out of it in a hurry. Did she look that dreadful? How horrible. She didn't want anybody to see her like this! She wanted to go home and start the afternoon all over again, beginning with the hairdresser at three.

In the emergency room, a very kind doctor cleaned her up briskly. "Mostly deep scratches, my dear," she said. "Nothing to leave a scar. I'm just going to put some stitches into this ankle and you'll be fine."

"Then I can still go to the dance tonight?" said Emily hopefully.

They all stared at her: doctor, nurse, aide.

"It's the first formal dance I've ever been to," she explained, feeling stupid. "I can go home and shower and put on another dress. I mean, it won't be a formal dress, but we can still go. I can catch up with Matt and we can limp in, don't you think?"

"Catch up with Matt," repeated a nurse slowly. She and the others exchanged glances. "Emily, we'd better make a few phone calls. You just lie here and we'll get your parents down."

Everybody else looked carefully at her damaged foot, and not at Emily.

Matt is dead, Emily thought.

The lightning missed me and got him. Half in, half out of that car the way he was. The wire must have been flung against him, or the lightning struck and he died, and they hadn't gotten

107

around to telling me yet. They'll wait until my mother and father are here.

Matt.

Nearly a stranger, but oh so close. So important!

Matt, who had liked her instantly. Thought her perfect from the first minute. Who got a special car, and special flowers to show that she, too, was special. Matt, who was able to make a good impression on her mother and father, who weren't all that impressed with Emily herself.

She was hardly aware of the stitching and bandaging on her foot.

When the doctor spoke to her she did not answer because she did not hear.

Matt was dead.

If she had not asked him to this dance. . . .

If she had remembered the first turn. . . .

Emily began to weep. I was worrying about my *hair!* she thought, wishing she could shave it all off. I ran worrying about my *dress!*

And Matt was out there dying.

Chapter 10

Kip caught a glimpse of Roddy. He was over by the refreshment tables. Kip had had the food spread out so that nobody would have to stand in line in order to eat. Roddy was standing against the food, as if on display. He was so clearly alone. His posture was one of defeat.

Do I look like that? Kip wondered. Am I standing on my side of the room, folded over as if I've a cramp in my side from running too fast?

It diminished her to watch Roddy. If I had come alone, she thought, at least it would have shown courage. People would have respected me for strength at least. But I came with a jerk, and that makes me something of a jerk as well. The minute I walk over and join him, I will be bracketed with him.

But the burden of standing alone was pressing in on her. Three hundred couples danced beneath her decorations, girls' heads lying on boys' shoulders. When the music stopped, conversation and laughter sparkled.

But not for Kip.

Swallowing, she followed the scarlet path around her fountain and her wooden swing and her rustic collections of apple barrels and pumpkin stacks. When she reached him, Roddy simply looked at her without speaking, making Kip feel more guilty than if she'd stuck a knife in between his ribs and watched him bleed.

Silently Roddy handed her a cup of punch and a tiny plate of food. The punch — something her mother often served; a ginger ale and lime sherbet mix — was not going over very well. The original sherbet was still floating around, looking like tired foam. The plate Roddy passed to her held one iced cookie (a donation from Veronica's mother, who evidently thought the dance was your usual flung-together jeans-and-disc-jockey kind of thing), one tiny crustless sandwich with an unidentifiable filling, one stuffed mushroom, hot on a toothpick, and one cheeseball, formerly hot.

The stuffed mushroom and cheeseball were from Gary's father's restaurant. Immediately she thought of Gary with Beth Rose. Amazing. Mechanically Kip said, "Thank you, Roddy."

No answer.

He didn't eat anything, either — just took the red toothpick out of his stuffed mushroom and pushed the bits of food around on his little paper plate. "Better not," advised Kip. "Everything will fall on the floor."

"Yeah," said Roddy. "I'm the kind of guy that happens to."

"You don't have to be," said Kip. "You could

be a little tougher than that, Roddy. Why did you let Molly and Christopher talk to you like that, anyhow? Why did you just wimp away?"

She could not believe she had said that. She — Kip — who was always kind, always understanding, always sympathetic. I deserve a smack, she thought.

Roddy put down his plastic glass of soda and his sagging paper plate. He folded his arms and stared at her across them. "What did you want me to do?" he demanded. "Toss a hand grenade into their car? Cut Christopher's phone line so he couldn't call Molly? Hit Molly, maybe, so she can't give me a hard time?"

Kip flushed. "Of course not," she said uneasily. "I just —"

"I know, I know," Roddy said, nodding and looking at the wall. "You pretend you don't want violence, but you crave it. You think I should be defending my honor and all that. I don't understand girls. You pretend you want somebody sensitive and understanding. That's a lot of junk. What you really want is a stupid, drunk, college kid like Christopher Vann."

"I don't, either! I wouldn't go out with Chris."

"You don't want to be out with me, either," Roddy said.

He flung the words at her like a weapon, and Kip, wanting to be peaceful, wanting to make friends, flung them right back instead. "You called me an hour before the dance. Did you think I would be thrilled or something?"

Roddy froze. After a bit he said, "Stupid, wasn't it?"

I am lower even than Molly, Kip thought. He knew Molly would be rotten to him. But he had every right to figure I would be nice.

Slowly Roddy moved away from her, giving her time, if she wanted it, to call him back, or to follow him and apologize. All her mother's training in good manners passed before Kip's eyes and all of it she chose not to bother with.

The thing is, Roddy, she thought after him, I don't like you! This is my dance and I want to be here with someone I like!

Roddy's slumped shoulders vanished in the press of dancers. Kip stood utterly alone, facing the cafeteria that she and she alone had transformed into a place of beauty with its aura of romance.

You win, world! Kip thought. I surrender. I'm sick of fighting. I'm sick of working every single minute to make people like me and failing.

Gary and Beth Rose passed her on their way to get something more to eat. "Just have to tell you again how much I'm enjoying your dance," Gary said to her, smiling his sweet smile.

She was not jealous of Beth. In her heart Kip knew that the only reasons she liked Gary were first his wonderful good looks and second his completely relaxed poise, as if he owned the cafeteria, and possibly the town. But Kip had tremendous ambition, and Gary had none, except to pitch in occasionally in his father's restaurant.

What's the answer? Kip thought. Am I constructed so that there is *not* a right boy for me? Is my personality the kind that won't let me fall in love? Or am I so busy being captain of this and chairman of that that boys don't know I'm a girl?

She had her car.

She could not seem to feel the slightest obligation to Roddy.

I'll just drive home, she thought. I admit it. This world is tougher than I am. I can't take another three hours of this.

Beth Rose kept thinking of her Aunt Madge's remark. "There's nothing quite so wonderful as a dance where every girl there is looking at you."

The dress is magic, Beth thought. For Aunt Madge it meant going with Virgil Hopkinson. For me it means Gary. Who is also magic.

"Come on," said Gary. "We've got to have pictures."

Beth Rose stared at him. Pictures? That cost so much.

"I've been keeping an eye on the photographer," said Gary. "If there's one thing I hate it's standing in line." Gary had his route through the crowd all picked out, and before Beth Rose had time to think about it, they were standing by the rose arbor.

Kip had gotten the garden center to loan her an actual arbor, and she'd twisted green twine around it, and felt leaves, and had pots of silk roses in bright pinks and reds and blushing scarlets. A tiny rustic seat for two slender people sat next to it. The seat wasn't quite big enough for two, so mostly the girl ended up sitting on the boy's lap.

Gary sat down first, taking up a lot of space, and grinned up at her. Her heart flopped over. He patted his knee, not the bench.

She was very, very aware of the couples around them. There must be a good twenty people whose conversations drifted to a halt, whose dance steps slowed, as they watched Gary and Beth Rose.

"Sit down, Beth," Gary said.

Beth sat. The old ivory lace that lined the neckline of her gown brushed against Gary's face. He looked down, then back at her, and they both flushed slightly, and ignored remarks from two giggling couples near them.

Fall in love with me, Gary! she thought. Please. Please sit here holding me and think there's nowhere on earth I'd rather be than here, and no girl I'd rather have in my lap than Beth Rose Chapman.

"All right, honey, move your arm a little this way," ordered the photographer. She moved her arm a little this way and she thought, Why ever move again? Why not just stay here in paradise with Gary?

They took one picture with Gary looking up into her face and another with both of them looking toward the photographer. One of the boys said, "Hey, Gary, you really need one of you scanning that neckline." And the photographer said, "Okay, let's have a kiss."

It was the first kiss of her life.

Nicer if he weren't obeying instructions, Beth Rose thought, and nicer if we were in private. But still. . . .

Gary's hand came up behind her head, and he tilted her head down ever so slightly, and strained up to reach her. The kiss was very light: a mere brush of the lips that would not even disturb her lipstick, but Beth Rose thought she would drift into the air, spun off into space by the pleasure of his touch.

Some of the kids started making remarks, but Beth hardly heard them. She slowly got off Gary's lap, wondering if she had been too heavy, or just right, and then Gary got up, and the photographer said, "That'll be a ten dollar deposit and another thirty when the photographs come in."

Beth froze. She had never expected it to cost that much. She had figured a quarter of that. Her heart fell as quickly as it had risen.

But not a moment of doubt crossed Gary's face. "Sure," he said, pulling a wallet out of his back pocket, handing over a ten, and taking the receipt. Beth watched the receipt being folded in half, tucked into the wallet. He can't forget me now, she thought. I'm in his wallet. I'm an investment. "Thank you," she said.

He just smiled.

Only reflex made Kip walk into the girls' room to check on her hair before she left. She was amused at herself in a dark and dreary way. You're leaving the dance, lady, she told herself. Now you worry about your hair? Nobody noticed you when you walked in, why should they notice you now?

She tried to remind herself of all the compliments she had had on her dance, but in the end only one compliment counted: to have a boy love her.

She felt so much like crying that it did not surprise Kip at all to walk in on sobs. They sounded rather like the sobs she was expecting from herself. In the row of mirrors, she could see nothing at all reflected in her face: not joy, not misery. In fact, she looked very nice.

I know what a formal dance is now.

Pretty dresses, desperate hearts.

Gradually she grew aware that somebody in this bathroom really was crying her heart out. Reluctantly, not really wanting to handle somebody else's agony when she was so busy with her own, Kip said, "Can I help?"

Pause. Then, whispery, fragile, "No, thank you."

The sobs were held under control. Kip waited, but nobody came out. "I'm going to leave the dance myself," Kip said tiredly. "If it's bad enough that you need a ride home, I'd be glad to take you."

More silence. Then, "Kip?" in a disbelieving voice.

"Yeah."

The door opened. And there stood Anne Stephens.

Nothing could have surprised Kip more.

Anne?

Whose life was perfect? Whose personality, talent, brains, figure, teeth, complexion, and style were all to be envied? Anne, standing hidden in the bathroom, sobbing until her mascara ran?

Probably had a fight with Con about something important, thought Kip sarcastically. Like whether to have tonight's photographs under the rose arbor or by the fountain.

"Oh, Kip," said Anne, her voice throaty from crying. Actually it sounded very attractive. Con probably told her he liked it. "Oh, Kip, I might have known it would be you. Not Con. Oh, no, Con wouldn't come after me. But I could count on you, Kip. You're so reliable."

Kip felt like smacking her. "So what's wrong?" she said. She really didn't care. Of all the adjectives she wanted to hear, *reliable* was the last. If Anne didn't need an ambulance or a ride home, Kip was bailing out. She wanted to go home and nurse her own hurts, not waste time over some pretend agony from a winner like Anne.

"I'm pregnant," said Anne.

For a moment the sentence meant nothing to Kip. She could not focus on it at all.

The distorted features of Anne's face seemed to shatter, and then come foggily back together, and what Kip saw there truly was agony. Not grief, not worry, not depression. *Agony.* "You're pregnant?" repeated Kip.

Anne nodded.

"Does Con know?"

"Yes. I told him when we got here."

Good for you, Kip thought. I myself would always time my tragic announcements for the entrance to my first formal dance. I hope you've learned from this, Anne old girl. Timing is all. "What did he say?" Kip asked.

"He got mad at me. He said he couldn't talk about it. It's my problem, he said. I was probably making it up, anyway, he said."

So this is what it's like to be the perfect couple, when the first thing goes wrong, Kip thought. Out loud she said, "We could cut him up in little pieces with a dull putty knife."

Anne nodded. "That has definitely passed through my mind. The problem is I love him. Anyhow, dead fathers aren't very useful."

Fathers.

To Kip the word "father" meant her own: forty, getting bald, teaching her to drive, gearing up to pay for her college tuition. But when Anne said "father" she meant Con. *Con!*

"I thought he'd come after me," said Anne. "I thought he'd want to be alone, too, and follow me out of the dance."

"This is the girls' bathroom," pointed out Kip. "No matter how much he wants to talk he won't follow you here."

"He won't follow me anywhere," said Anne dully.

"Do your parents know? Does anybody else know?"

"Only Con." Anne leaned against the wall. How thin she looked. Kip found her eyes floating toward Anne's waist, and lower, trying to imagine both the conception and creation of a real person who was half Anne, half Con. Kip couldn't. Could Anne? Did Anne feel different inside? Could she feel this little person — or was it just cells bunched up together, presenting more problems than Anne knew how to handle?

If you wanted to go that way, there was one easy solution. If Anne felt like it, the whole thing could be ended without her parents and grandmother ever knowing.

But those were questions Kip could not quite manage.

"I haven't told my parents and my grandmother," whispered Anne. "They think I'm perfect. They'll hate me. And Con won't be with me when I have to tell them. He's mad at me. That's his only response to this. Mad at me, as if I'm the only one around, and he didn't do a thing. Oh, Kip, I trusted him completely to be the most important person in my life — and now I know differently. Whatever decision I make — whatever I do about this pregnancy — he won't be there. *I'll be alone.*"

That's the sentence, Kip thought. That's the one we're all so scared of. It isn't the being pregnant that panics her as much as the being alone. And do I know how that feels! Worst punishment on earth, I suppose, to be alone. Wounds don't heal without friends and love.

"Oh, Anne," she said softly. "Oh, Anne, I'm so sorry. It sounds so awful."

Anne began to cry again, terrible sobs that

came out of her as if attached to her lungs: sobs that came protesting, bleeding, wrenched from Anne's throat.

She clung to Kip, because there was no other help there. What if somebody walks in on us like this? thought Kip, trying to comfort Anne with pats and hugs — Anne whose life was a shambles, for whom the only good hug would be one from Con.

She had a slight sense that maybe the door *had* just opened.

While Anne sobbed, had Kip heard a creak? Had there been a click while Anne talked?

Kip looked over her shoulder. The bathroom door was closed. It was much too heavy and too tight to listen through.

But had somebody already been there?

And edged out, not wanting to witness a scene?

Or heard it all . . . and left . . . hugging the gossip to herself, ready to spread across a roomful of fascinated listeners?

Chapter 11

Emily's father brought her favorite jeans, her favorite slate blue cotton turtleneck, and her beloved gray-blue tweed pullover with the cables. She'd worn this so often it was practically a uniform.

"I don't know if those jeans will pull up over the bandage," said the nurse doubtfully, but Emily had no trouble. The pant legs were wider than they were fashionable.

Emily stared at herself in the mirror.

She was dull and bedraggled. Her hair, vigorously toweled by one of the aides, was nearly dry, and hung the way it always did when given no attention: nearly straight, but not quite. A wrinkled look, actually, as though there was something wrong with her.

No makeup. No color whatsoever in her cheeks. No eyelashes, of course, because Emily's were invisible without mascara.

And because she always wore those jeans and sweater, she looked faded, as if she'd been standing there for years in the same clothes.

"Okay, sweetie," said her father when she was dressed, and in front of all the emergency room staff, he hugged her. Emily was surprised. He was undemonstrative at the best of times, and she could not remember a hug in front of people.

Slowly she was aware that he hardly noticed all these other people. He was looking only at her. This is the way Anne Stephens' family always looks, Emily thought. This is how it feels to have your parent look at you and think you're perfect.

But oh, the price!

"You saved a man's life," her father said. "I know how scared you've always been of lightning. I have to admit, Emily, it always annoyed me."

The young woman doctor looked very sympathetic. The two nurses paused to listen.

Emily thought of death.

In English class it seemed to her half the poems, plays, and stories they studied dealt with death. She had written essays about it, and analyzed some poet's view of it. But now she knew she had never given death a moment's thought.

She tried to feel Matt as dead.

Gone.

Forever gone. Transformed, perhaps into something else — or simply vanished, as if he had never been.

She could not grasp it. It loomed before her: horrific, strong, terrible — yet meaningless. How could death possibly have anything to do with her, Emily, in blue jeans and a cable knit sweater?

"Oh, sweetie, I'm so proud of you," said her father huskily, and he hugged her again, and this time his arms stayed around her. The hug didn't scare him off the way it usually did. He kept on hugging, as if to preserve his daughter from the death she, too, had nearly had.

Emily began to cry.

"Because you went through the lightning to save him, honey," said her father. "Through the dark. Never thinking about your own safety, or what would happen to you if you got hit. You just ran, and saved the fellow's life."

"But Daddy, I did worry!" Emily burst out. "I was so scared. Every moment I was terrified. I was crying. And it was my dress I was worried about, not that man. I wasn't a heroine. I just did it by accident. And I was never brave."

It was the doctor who hugged her this time. "That's what courage is, Emily. To keep going when you're scared. To sacrifice your dress, when the dress really matters, because that's what you have to do. I'm impressed, too." The doctor smiled gently. "And proud."

"You don't even know me," said Emily, weeping again.

"Oh, but we do know you. We've seen you at the worst moment of your life, Emily, and you're wonderful. We love you."

Emily stared at the doctor. She means it, Emily thought. She loves me. It is possible to love a person you've known only for a minute, someone whose life is completely unknown to

you. She *is* proud of me. As if I represented —
oh — humanity, or something!

"Not as much as I love you," Matt's voice
said.

Emily looked up.

Matt, grinning, his hair standing up damp
and bristly like a porcupine. Matt, not a scratch
on him. Matt, wearing clothing that looked
totally wrong yet oddly familiar.

Emily's father and the doctor let go of her,
and Matt bounded forward to give Emily an
extremely tight hug. She gasped. He hugged
her as if shaking hands with an important
person: like sealing a bond.

"Matt. I thought you were dead."

"Me? Why would I be dead?"

For the life of her, Emily could not remember
why she had come to the conclusion that he was.
But who cares? she thought. What matters now
is that Matt is alive! Alive — and —

And I look awful. The worst of my life. "I
look awful," said Emily.

The entire room full of people began to laugh:
doctor, father, nurses' aides, and Matt.

Emily glared at them. "It's true," she said
huffily. "After all that energy spent on fixing
my hair and getting the perfect dress, I look
awful."

"What matters is, how do you feel?" said
Matt.

"Pretty good."

"Then let's go on to the dance."

"I'm wearing blue jeans," she protested. "It's
a formal dance."

"So? We certainly have good excuses for looking like this. My father and grandfather are driving down to get the Ford. Dad'll drive on home in his car and Granddad will drive the Ford home, so we don't have to worry about the car."

Emily could truly say she had never worried about the car. All she could think of was facing people like Anne Stephens or Molly Nelmes, who would look fantastic, when Emily, who was rather plain to start with, now had nothing going for her at all.

"My foot is totally anesthetized," she said slowly. "I could probably dance all night and never know it."

The doctor snorted. "You'd know it in the morning," she said. "If you really feel up to attending the dance, sit down all evening with your foot elevated, is that clear?"

"We'll be fine as long as my pants don't fall down," said Matt.

Emily stared at him.

"They're your father's jeans," he explained. "And your father's shirt, sweater, shoes, and socks. All a little big. I'm sort of wading as I walk."

"Well, that settles it. I cannot go to the first formal of my entire life with a man who is wading in his clothing and my hair is wrinkled," said Emily, not very clearly.

"Sure you can." Matt was grinning from ear to ear: a big sloppy puppy grin, his eyes crinkled to nothing. It wiped Emily out, of course. "Heroines can do anything," Matt told her.

"People love them in spite of it. Heroines can carry off anything in public, and people are just filled with respect."

I'm a heroine? thought Emily. "No, you were a hero," she corrected him. "You were the one who actually saved his life."

"You can argue about it in the car," said Mr. Edmundson. "If I'm the one driving you two around, I'd like to get started."

Emily saw herself reflected in her father's and Matt's eyes. I did go through the storm, she thought. I did conquer the thing I'm most afraid of on earth. And I am with a boy who thinks I'm pretty wonderful.

She gave Matt her arm. "Wade on," she said, and they laughed together, and Matt kissed her and this time it was not a kiss of fear, or comfort, or relief.

It was a kiss of love.

Beth and Gary left the rose arbor very slowly, his arm around her waist, consciously on exhibit. People grinned at them, and Beth smiled back, feeling like Princess Diana acknowledging the waves of her loyal subjects. Gary wanted to find Con and Anne again. Fine with Beth. There was certainly no nicer pair in the school.

When they found Con, he was standing halfway between the band and the food, as if stranded.

"What's the matter?" Gary asked.

"Anne disappeared," Con said irritably.

"Probably found somebody better," Gary said

cheerfully. It was something easy to say, since in this case it was so impossible.

Con laughed.

Oh to be that close! Beth Rose thought. To know that the person you love could not possibly find anybody better than you.

She sat quietly. Con and Gary talked. They both enjoyed car racing and they'd been up at the same stock car race in Waterford, without seeing each other. "Anne go with you to that?" asked Gary with interest. "Most girls don't usually like that stuff."

Beth wanted to say that *she* liked that stuff, but then Gary would want to know what car races she'd been to, and the answer was "none." Or then again he might say, "Well, then, you and I will have to go sometime, huh, Beth?" And Con would smile, too, and say, "You two going out now?" and Gary would say . . . .

But Gary was still talking to Con, and Beth had not spoken, and the conversation was all her private fantasy.

I'm tired of fantasy, Beth thought. I'd like a little reality for a change.

"Beth," said Con, rather sharply, as if she had offended.

Beth jumped.

"Listen," he said. Again rather sharply, as if he was accusing her of purposely not listening to him.

"Anne's been in the girls' room forever," Con said. "Would you go see if she's sick or something?" He frowned. "She felt kind of crummy earlier this evening."

Beth was struck by his tone of voice. He sounded more annoyed than worried, as if Anne feeling crummy was a real nuisance. She put the thought away. She loved thinking of Anne and Con together. She didn't want a single feeling that their relationship was less than perfect. When *I* have a boyfriend, it'll be perfect, she told herself.

"Sure," she said. "I'll be back in a minute."

She got up.

Gary smiled at her vaguely. He and Con went back to discussing race cars.

And Beth knew she was making a fatal mistake. As long as she was right there, Gary would stay with her. He was too courteous to abandon her outright — or possibly too lazy. But once she walked out of his sight . . . he would be gone.

She did not know how she knew this.

After all, until a few hours ago she had known Gary only by sight and reputation. As for the beginning of the evening, it still had a dreamlike quality; the two hours had slid by with such speed it was difficult to believe the big white and black clock on the cafeteria wall.

Thirty feet away from the boys, Beth Rose stopped walking, and looked back. Be watching me, Gary! she begged.

But he was not.

Out of sight, out of mind, she thought. No matter how graceful I feel, no matter how perfectly this dress fits me, no matter how beautifully Aunt Madge fixed my hair, he still isn't watching. He's a hundred times more important to me than I am to him.

Go back right now, Beth Rose, she told herself. Go back. Forget about finding Anne. If there was ever a girl at Westerly High who could take care of herself it's Anne Stephens. You walk away now, you'll lose Gary because he'll forget about you. You'll be alone.

But she could think of no excuse to give Con or Gary for returning without having looked for Anne.

She kept walking toward the girls' room, and the next time she glanced over her shoulder, there were too many of Kip's autumn props between her and the boys to see Gary.

Three people stopped her to tell her how lovely she looked.

Don't chat with me, I have to hurry! thought Beth Rose, edging away from them. But they were special people—important people—people she had always yearned to be friends with: Pammy, and Caitlin, and Sue, and their dates. Such nice girls! And she knew they had noticed her because of Gary.

Quick. Run get Anne, throw her back in Con's arms, sit down next to Gary before he's gone, she thought.

"And the lace," said Sue enthusiastically. "I just love that lace."

"Is it supposed to be gray?" Caitlin asked.

"I'm sure it was always gray," said Sue immediately. "I think pink and gray is such a sophisticated combination. I love it on you, Beth Rose."

They smiled at Beth, as if conferring honors on her. *You, too, are sophisticated, like us.* She wanted to stay with them forever, being one of their crowd, laughing with them, talking about clothes with them, as if she belonged.

But she had other things to do. When Sue and Caitlin finally turned back to their very bored dates (few boys in the room cared whether lace was ivory or gray) Beth Rose whirled to get to the bathroom.

And bumped into Christopher Vann.

"I'm sorry," she muttered, hardly glancing at him, trying to steer around him.

He stepped the same direction she did, so that she had to move back again. He did the same. "Sorry," she mumbled again, blushing. She knew that Caitlin and Sue were watching, and amused by her clumsiness. And with Molly's date, of all people!

But the next time it happened she knew he was doing it on purpose, like an obnoxious fourth grader. She looked up at him. And up some more. He was very tall. And very wide.

And very drunk.

" 'Lo there, my dear," he said to Beth Rose. "Great dress. I like your dress. Better than Molly's old rag."

Beth did not dare look at Molly to check whether her dress really was an old rag. "Nonsense," said Beth. "Molly looks beautiful." She angled past. Christopher didn't let her.

"Excuse me, please," she said to him.

"Where you going?" he demanded loudly. He

put his hand on her shoulder. A little lower than her shoulder, but not quite on her breast.

She would have expected anger, but the emotion that came to her was fear. She hated his hand touching her. It frightened her, the way it lay there, large and possessive.

"Chrissie, let's dance," said Molly quickly.

Beth Rose wasn't being rescued; Molly just didn't like Christopher's affections — if that was the word — going elsewhere.

"Don't wanna dance," said Christopher, shaking his head several times. Like a cow about to moo, thought Beth Rose.

"I'm dancing with this girl," he said to Molly. "I like her dress best. This is Harvard stuff, this dress. Yours came off some damn discount rack. Her dress here, this is the real thing. You look at this girl, Molly, you take lessons from her."

Beth Rose was afraid even to glance at Molly to see how Molly took that.

"In fact, I think this dress would look better without all the lace," said Christopher, and his hand closed on the fabric that gently gathered just above her breasts.

She was afraid to jerk away because then the dress would definitely tear, and afraid not to — because Christopher was enjoying himself enough to go ahead and rip the dress right in front of the whole room.

She just knew that Sue and Caitlin and their dates were staring. "Let go or I'll kick you," Beth hissed.

Christopher laughed happily. "I like that in a girl," he said, nodding.

"Now Chrissie, there isn't all that much to explore on Beth," said Molly, slithering in between them. "You're not deserting your cute little Gary so soon, are you, Bethie? Well, I don't suppose you can desert him faster than he deserts you."

Beth stared at her. "What do you mean?"

Molly laughed. "Gary hasn't got much of an attention span. From one girl to another, Beth, he isn't even a one-night stand. More of a one-dance stand, if you ask me."

Christopher let go of Beth's dress. He put his heavy hand on Molly instead. Beth Rose shuddered and ducked under Christopher's arm. "For *you* he was probably a one-night stand, Moll," said Christopher. "For whatshername he might last longer. Girls like Anne Stephens. I like her. Probably would last with a girl like Anne Stephens. Pretty girl."

"Pretty pregnant," said Molly clearly.

Beth left as fast as she could.

Chapter 12

Anne had never meant to deceive anybody. She was an open, happy person, and if somebody had asked her, when she was fourteen, if she would make a career of lying to her family, she would have been shocked.

She was still shocked.

Perhaps the reason she got away with it was because Anne still thought of herself as the kind of girl who would never lie to her mother.

The reason it was so easy was the way Con's family lived. If they were almost finished restoring the house they lived in, then his mother was sure to have bought a new house, and be spending all her time there working with the carpenters or consulting with the furnace men. If they'd just moved into the new house, and it was filled with masons and floor-refinishers, probably the old house was not yet sold . . . and probably Con still had his key.

We're going bowling, Mom.

That's nice, honey. Have a good time.

Parts of it were good. She did love Con. But

letting themselves into a vacant house, where the heat was turned off and the furniture was gone, using the football blanket from the trunk of the car, going afterwards to the bathroom with no towels, no soap?

Anne cringed thinking about it.

Once they got caught by a realtor showing a family through the house. When they heard the key turn in the lock downstairs, they were up and leaping into their clothes in a heartbeat. Anne would not have thought zippers and buttons could close so quickly. Con was down the steps before the potential buyers got to the kitchen, smiling at the realtor, saying he was trying to find a hammer he'd left behind.

"Oh, we'll keep our eyes open for it," said the man who was thinking of buying the house.

"It's a special one," said Con. "It was my first one. My grandfather gave it to me when I was about seven. You'll know it because it has a very worn wooden handle."

Con's grandfather had died before Con was born, but it made a good line. Anne got the blanket folded and slipped out of the house into Con's car, and nobody even knew she was there.

Con's parents never noticed where he was or wasn't. They let Con make his own decisions. By and large, he made good ones. Anne should know. She was always part of them.

She thought about Con's decisions.

He was the one who chose whether or not to spend time with Anne. She was the one who waited, and after she knew what he planned, built her own plans around them.

How reasonable it had always seemed!

Con did not smother her, the way her mother and grandmother did, nor did she smother Con. She and Con rarely argued, never fought. Now she realized why. She had never demanded anything of him. All by himself, he was charming, funny, interesting, and *there*. But when had she ever asked for more?

I've dated him for three years, Anne thought, and slept with him for one, and now for the first time I see that I don't know him.

Her mind ran over any other disagreements they'd ever had. Con liked things to go smoothly. Whenever things got the least little bit rough, he'd buy his way out. "We'll go into town and shop for those earrings you like," he'd tell her. Somehow she would forget about the argument, or else it would seem too petty to resurrect.

Besides, weren't the earrings — and the bangle bracelet, and the gold necklace — weren't they proof of Con's love?

Now she thought they were not proof of anything at all, except that Con didn't want to argue, and happened to have some cash.

What would happen if we *had* to argue? she thought.

Because this time we *have* to. I don't know what I think. I don't know what I want. I don't know what is the best thing to do. I want to hear what he says and I want to thrash it out.

Kip said, "Anne, I just can't believe that Con will dump you. He's too terrific a person. He loves you too much."

"He loves me a lot," said Anne slowly, "but

I'm afraid when the going gets tough, Con will simply sail on smoother waters."

Kip was upset by that. "I should think you'd have more faith in him than that," she said, thinking, *Three years?* Three years she's given to this guy and made love with him and she doesn't know whether he's good, bad, or indifferent?

Anne felt old. Oh, so much older than Kip! How to explain that until now she had had nothing but faith?

Perhaps faith was a thing you didn't know if you had until it was tested.

Anne washed her face with a paper towel. In the harsh fluorescent light of the bathroom, she and Kip examined her makeup. "This is my only slip-up," Kip told Anne. "I meant to get new lighting in here before the dance."

Anne had to laugh. "Oh, Kip," she said, hugging her, "I feel so much better. Isn't that crazy? But just telling you and I'm better."

I'm better, too, thought Kip. I don't like the position I'm in, but I *really* don't like the position you're in. She said, "I can see why you would tell me. I mean, girls share things. But why on earth did you tell Con *tonight* and ruin the evening? I should think you would have told him earlier or later, but not now."

Anne shrugged. "Kip, my whole *life* may be ruined. Who cares about one stupid dance?"

One stupid dance.

Kip turned to hide her face. This is *my* dance, she thought. My bouquet thrown to romance. Only no boy noticed. But it's still a special dance, and I'm still proud of it. It's not stupid.

Kip forgot they were in a bathroom with mirrors. She couldn't hide her face; Anne read it all, and was stabbed with remorse. "I'm sorry. You did your usual perfect job, Kip. The dance isn't stupid, it's lovely. *I'm* the one who's stupid."

"You really think Con will walk out on you?" Kip asked wistfully, wanting it to be untrue, unfair. When I find a man, he will be a loyal man. I would never fall for the kind of person who doesn't have the most important things: loyalty and kindness and pride.

"He could be gone right now," Anne said. And then she laughed slightly. "But after all, Kip, why would a person stay to cope with a pregnancy if he didn't have to? *I* would certainly walk away if *I* could."

The door opened.

Anne immediately turned to face the mirror, and pretended to be fixing her hair. She had neither comb nor brush, so Kip fished in her own tiny purse and handed her a pocket comb.

Beth Rose Chapman came up to them.

"Hi, Beth," said Anne easily. "Honestly, Kip, don't you just love Beth's dress? It's the loveliest gown at the dance."

Oh, Anne, thought Kip ruefully, you mean well, but you really know how to zap it to a person. I wouldn't mind having you say that *I* have the loveliest gown at the dance. Of course it wouldn't be true, but I'd still like to hear it. She said out loud, smiling at Beth, "It sure is."

Beth looked breathless, and rather upset.

Oh, no, thought Kip, shrinking away, not another Person In Distress. Don't tell me your problems, Beth, I can't stand it. Remind me not to become a family counselor. I don't have enough care to go around.

"Con's worried about you, Anne. He sent me to get you."

Kip could never have predicted the reaction that would bring. Here she and Anne had spent the last fifteen minutes sobbing about how Con was probably pretty rotten beneath the surface, and here Anne had actually admitted she didn't expect a single thing from him . . . and the comb hung forgotten in her hand. A smile began at the edges of her lips, and spread across her face, lighting her eyes, putting color in her cheeks. "He did?" she said happily.

Oh, Anne! thought Kip, and this time it was Kip who was older, and wiser, and sadder. How thrilled Anne was that Con had sent a messenger to fetch her. How quickly she forgot that she didn't trust Con. One word from Con and she was his again.

Women, thought Kip. We're all crazy.

Anne, perfect Anne.

Anne, who was too good to smile at Molly when they walked into the dance together.

Anne, who was too special to share a laugh with Molly.

Anne, who marched to the far side of the cafeteria so she wouldn't have to stand near Christopher and Molly.

Anne was pregnant and thought Con would dump her.

Molly loved it. The irony! How richly deserved it was! Perfect people deserved to get hurt. It was so annoying the way some people's lives were always smooth and serene. A wrinkle in Anne's life. Molly liked that. And not just a wrinkle, either. Being pregnant at seventeen and not married and being deserted — you had to call that the Grand Canyon of problems.

Here Molly had planned the perfect evening herself. She'd dumped jerky Roddy, and found Christopher, and was expecting a perfect evening with a Harvard man and what did she get? A stupid, rude fool who made passes at other girls because he was tanked up to the top with cheap wine, or something that smelled like it. Miracle the chaperones even let them in.

Beth Rose tiptoed away like a skittish animal. Molly timed her last remark just loud enough for Beth to hear. And did Beth ever hear. The girl was a lousy actress. Beth jumped a foot, pretended she hadn't, practically ran into the wall instead of the door, and had to use her hands to feel her way out of the cafeteria. *That* was what you called a real reaction.

Molly giggled to herself.

Beth Rose would tell Gary, and — Well, no. Gary probably wouldn't tell a soul. She had never known someone as detached as Gary. Either he really didn't listen to stories, or he really didn't care, or he instantly forgot them, because Gary never told anybody anything.

Molly had a suspicion that he was too thick even to gossip. It never occurred to her that he loathed gossip, and walked instantly away from it. But if she had known, she would have liked that, too: hoping that Beth Rose would ruin *her* evening by saying the wrong things to the wrong person.

Christopher said, "Starving."

You slob, she thought. You're down to one-word sentences now. She put her hands on her hips and glared at him. "Okay. You go get something to eat, Chrissie. I'll catch up to you in a minute. I have to talk to somebody."

Christopher lurched toward the food. For a minute, Molly kept an eye on him, but he didn't pause to talk to anybody. Good. She was a little worried about what he was going to say or do next. What if he talked to a parent chaperone the way he had to Beth Rose?

She went up to Sue and Caitlin.

Sue was one of those girls who had been suave, sophisticated, and casual since kindergarten. Always in the popular group, always with a great-looking boyfriend, Sue gave parties to which Molly had never been invited. Anne was always invited, of course. Anne was always invited everywhere. Anne, who couldn't be bothered to speak to Molly.

Sue was with Jimmy. Jimmy was not the brightest person in the world, but he was certainly one of the nicest. Everybody said so, but Molly had never had a chance to test Jimmy. She couldn't help checking him out, even while she talked to his date.

Caitlin was an unknown to Molly. Caitlin had moved to town a year before and was not in any of Molly's classes, even gym or typing or study. Slightly chubby, with thick, badly cut hair, she had a great pealing laugh that shook entire rooms and made everybody jump in astonishment and then burst out laughing with her. Molly did not think Caitlin had a single thing to offer except that bizarre laugh, but evidently this was enough, because Sue adopted Caitlin almost the day she moved to Westerly.

Molly resented that, too. She, Molly, had been in the wings her whole life. Who was Caitlin to march in and enter Sue's circle just like that?

Caitlin's date was a boy Molly had never even seen before, and she gave him a quick assessment and decided he was another nothing, like Roddy.

"Hi, there, Sue," said Molly, ignoring Caitlin and the boys.

Sue smiled. "Hi, Molly. I see Christopher is a little under the weather."

Molly would gladly have slapped Sue for that. She drew in a breath, ready to fight with words at least, but Sue's next words were balm to Molly's soul. "I guess these college guys really start partying and they can't stop," said Sue. "I always wanted to date a Harvard man. Has Christopher talked to you about it much? I would adore going to Boston. I hear it's such a great college town. My mother thinks I should apply to school there."

Molly beamed at her. "I'll probably go there

for a college weekend," she said, although Christopher had not said a single word about it. Immediately Molly could imagine the whole weekend: Harvard Yard, teams rowing on the river, the Boston Common and Paul Revere, and a football game where everybody drove Mercedes and had tailgate picnics with the wine in real crystal. I'm ready, Molly thought.

"Ooooh," Sue said. "A weekend? How great!"

"Boston," Caitlin said meditatively. "I went there for a week once. We went to about a thousand historical houses and whaling museums and stuff."

"How awful," Molly said, who liked buildings only if they sold clothing inside.

"Harvard, huh?" said Caitlin's date. "I didn't know anybody from this school ever got into Harvard."

"Oh, he's terribly smart," Molly said quickly, although Christopher's actions did not really support this statement. "But I really need to talk about something else." She looked apologetically at the boys and didn't bother to look at Caitlin at all. "Do you have a minute, Sue?"

Sue looked surprised, but she said sure, and detached herself.

Anne Stephens, you stupid fool, Molly thought, you won't snub me again in a hurry. You're such a jerk. You go get A plus in every subject and you don't catch on to the most important one of all. You think school really matters, Anne? You've got eight or nine months now to find out what *really* matters.

In a very low voice, Molly said, "It's Anne. I think she may need your help."

Sue looked amazed, as well she might. Anne always had Con around to help her. "What's the matter?" Sue asked blankly.

"Well," said Molly, dragging it out because Caitlin was getting curious. She might as well have another mouth to spread the rumor, even if she didn't like Caitlin. "Well, I don't want to interfere, or anything, but. . . ."

Caitlin drifted over to them. Molly smiled enough to include her, and Caitlin joined them.

"I was in the bathroom," Molly said confidingly, "and I heard Anne crying. Now I know Anne isn't crazy about me, so I didn't get involved, and besides, Kip was with her, but Anne was telling Kip that she's pregnant and Con has left her to face it alone."

Sue's entire face became slack with shock.

Caitlin sucked in her breath.

Ten feet away Sue's date Jimmy said, "Hurry up, girls. I like this song. I want to dance."

"Not now," Sue said vaguely.

"You'd better go help her," Molly said.

Caitlin not only did not know Molly, she had never set eyes on her before. But there was something slimy about this girl. Molly's hair was lovely, her dress was attractive, her speech was pleasant — and yet Caitlin instinctively did not trust her. "Are you exaggerating, Molly?" she asked quietly.

"No!" Molly looked offended. "Anne's so upset she's practically ready to open her wrists."

Molly's face grew sad and concerned.

"Oh, my God," said Sue to Caitlin. "Come on!"

The girls took off for the bathroom without even giving reasons to their dates. Naturally the boys were confused and more than a little annoyed, and naturally they wanted to know what Molly had said to make this happen.

"Oh, I really can't say," Molly said sadly. "It was very private. It was— well — well, I think I could trust the two of you." She smiled. She told them, too. It was a thoroughly enjoyable few minutes. She left them in speechless surprise and drifted on.

Winding around pumpkins and split rail fences and apple barrels, she thought how weird Kip was to have chosen that kind of stuff for a formal dance. She, Molly, would have gone in for glass and glitter and sleek surfaces and gaudy lights. But it was nice, because it divided the people into little groups whether they wanted this or not, and each little group had at least one person Molly could say a word to. She forced herself to stop after the third time. Best if the rumor spread through other lips now. She didn't want it all at her door.

Not, Molly thought virtuously, that it really is a rumor. It's the truth. Didn't I hear Anne say so herself? If she wants it kept a deep dark secret she shouldn't go talking about it in the girls' room.

So there.

Miss Perfect.

Hah.

Chapter 13

Sue's mind was a blur of panic and clarity. She must get to the bathroom, stop Anne, call for help, kill Con Winters, telephone Anne's mother. . . .

She and Caitlin ran into the bathroom.

There stood Kip, leaning against the mirrors, her arms folded, a pensive expression on her face.

There was Beth Rose, bending over slightly, while Anne fixed a hairpin that had come loose in Beth's braids.

"There," Anne said with satisfaction. "That should hold it, Beth." Anne looked up, saw Sue and Caitlin, and smiled at them. A real smile. A happy smile. Sue had known Anne too long to get confused on that score.

This was simply a girls' room, with three girls, peacefully fixing their hair. Sue didn't know what to say. She had believed Molly; she still believed Molly; and yet —

Caitlin had a brisk personality. She said,

"Listen, I'm just going to leap in where angels fear to tread."

"You're going to do what?" Kip said.

"Fools leap in where angels fear to tread," Caitlin quoted.

Anne looked mildly interested in this idea; Beth Rose looked totally blank, and Kip said, "Oh, I didn't know. Thank you, Caitlin."

Sue and Caitlin looked at each other.

Sue shrugged.

"And?" said Kip, smiling.

Caitlin managed a laugh. "And that is the end of a long conversation Sue and I were having. About us." Caitlin looked into the mirror, as if she had come into the bathroom for that purpose. Actually she hated mirrors and bathrooms, because she thought she was very plain, and she hated proof.

Sue said, "I am very gullible, Kip. Some day they're going to give a Gullible Person of the Week Award, and I'll win fifty-two in a row."

"You can't have that many," said Beth Rose. "I feel sure I can win more than you can."

They all laughed. Sue thought, Beth Rose has possibilities. And then Sue thought, Anne doesn't *look* pregnant.

Caitlin thought, Anne doesn't look suicidal.

Anne said, "I'm *so* disappointed. Here I was absolutely sure I had that trophy all sewed up and now I find I have a roomful of competition."

They all laughed again, and all of them except Beth pretended to have makeup to fix, and then they exited in a group, with Sue and Caitlin lingering slightly, and keeping to the rear.

Sue muttered, "Let's go kill Molly."

"Sounds good to me."

"Bad enough she should spread rumors that Anne is pregnant and Con is a worthless rat — but to imply Anne is killing herself? Somebody should lock Molly up. She is really filth."

Anne was practically running on ahead of them — definitely not the picture of a girl abandoned by her boyfriend. Beth Rose was trotting to keep up.

"What infuriates me is," Sue said, "I really and truly believed Molly. I was actually planning what I would say to Anne's mother on the phone, so that she wouldn't kill herself, too!"

They laughed from embarrassment, terribly relieved that nothing was wrong with Anne and terribly angry that Molly had dared anything like that. And inside Sue still felt a thread of panic. Surely Molly had had something to base her remarks on! But Kip — Kip was there. You *knew* you could rely on Kip. If something really was wrong, Kip would fix it. Tentatively Sue said, "We could ask Kip. What do you think?"

"I think the less said about this the better," Caitlin said.

They paused because Sue was having trouble with her heels. The shoes were fractionally too large; she had bought them on a hot day, she was thinking, when her feet were swollen. She slipped around inside them, and the hem of her long gown kept getting caught inside her shoe, and tripping her from behind. It was infuriating because it made Sue feel like a stumbling giraffe.

On the other side of the rose arbor, they overheard a very quiet conversation from the chaperones.

"Well, I suppose a certain amount of nasty behavior is understandable," said one mother. "If *I* were thrown out of Harvard, I'd be in a pretty bad mood myself."

"If *I* were thrown out of Harvard," said the father, "I'd be crawling back begging for forgiveness, not being drunk and disorderly at some high school dance."

"That filth Molly," Sue said to Jimmy, as soon as he came over to her. "Did she tell you a bunch of lies about Anne?"

Jimmy had never been so relieved in his life. Con was a good friend of his. He didn't want to have to think about Con's situation, or Con's reaction to it, or what would happen to Anne no matter what. "Yes, but we didn't believe a word of it," Jimmy said. "Molly's a fake. Always has been."

Sue beamed at him. "Come on," she said. "We're following Molly around the cafeteria."

"Last person on earth I'd follow anywhere," Jimmy protested.

"We have counter rumors to spread," Sue said. She and Caitlin laughed insanely, and of course half of the dancers turned to listen to Caitlin, and to wonder what was going on now.

"Beth Rose," said Anne, in greeting, as she came into the ladies' room.

Beth smiled at her, praying that Anne would

somehow escape the rumor Molly was spreading. How can I keep Anne from hearing it? she wondered. And if Con hears what Molly's saying, he might kill her. Or Christopher. Which they both deserve, but still. . . .

"Con sent me to get you," Beth Rose said. She thought, I just *know* Molly went and said the same thing to Sue and Caitlin.

All the emotion Anne had felt in the last quarter of an hour with Kip evaporated. Both panic and calm, both knowledge and fear. She was exactly what she had been a few weeks ago: in love with Con Winter. Blossoming into a wide joyous smile, like a girl on her first date, she cried, "Really? He sent you to get me?" And the next thing Beth knew, Anne was fussing happily with Beth's hair, and talking about how they would have to double date — she with Con, Beth with Gary — when in flew Sue and Caitlin.

Beth knew in a moment what Sue and Caitlin had heard, and she felt for them, stumbling around, trying to save them from the worst possible *faux pas.*

"Let's go back to the boys," Anne said happily. She and Beth Rose rushed down the hall, past the rose arbor, past the pumpkin stack, past the old wooden swing and the scarecrow she had not noticed before, leaning at a crazy angle against two sheaves of corn. Why are we running? Beth Rose thought. She looked at Anne, and Anne's face was bright and gay and almost feverish.

The band was playing a very slow piece, and

most of the room was dancing: no steps, just close swaying, eyes half closed, hands tightly clasped. Anne and Beth Rose were going at top speed, so that they seemed to be out of synchronization with the rest of the world.

Then they were with the boys and Anne was babbling, too many words, too fast, and even Beth could see it was wrong; it didn't fit and Anne was making Con irritable.

She realized that while all the girls were struggling to soothe the boys, none of the boys seemed to be struggling in return.

This falling in love stuff is a one way street, she thought. The boys are just sauntering along the pavement and they're willing to have us walk beside them if the sun is shining, but —

"Let's dance, Beth Rose," said Gary, and all her thoughts were forgotten: swept away by Gary like a wisp of cloud by a storm. He was too much for her, and her emotions toward him were too much. She dismissed every thought but the thoughts of his masculinity and his nearness. She began daydreaming of what would happen between them.

He'll be crazy about me by the time the evening's over. He'll pull me off into that corner over there behind the scarecrow. The chaperones haven't noticed it. You slip behind the corn sheaves and you're private in the shadows. We'll kiss. Then he'll really be in love with me.

He'll ask me out.

He'll ask me for next Friday night, but he won't be able to stand the wait. He'll telephone me Sunday noon to ask if I liked the dance as much as he did. He'll drive over Sunday afternoon. We'll sit and talk and then we'll go for a drive. And we'll park out by the reservoir near the Nature Preserve and we'll kiss and hug and go crazy. And I'll invite him for supper on Monday and he'll say, Oh, let's have pizza out instead and. . . .

Anne's heart was beating as if she was on a blind date with a sexy stranger. But it almost is, she thought, taking the familiar hand, resting her head on the familiar shoulder. As Gary and Beth Rose moved out onto the dance floor, Anne and Con began dancing very slowly right where they stood. Anne felt so reassured! How could she have doubted Con? Kip was right; it was a disgrace that she had surrendered her belief in him after two sentences, two minutes.

His strong heavy arms wrapped around her like protection from all storms. She smiled at him, their eyes locking the way they always did, and his were filled with the affection she had always felt from him.

Oh, Con, how I love you, she thought. "Listen, Con," she said. "I'm sorry I threw that at you so fast. I know it's hard to believe. The test was six days ago and I've been reeling from the shock ever since. And I know the dance is fun, but Con, tonight I can't have fun. We have to talk."

She had gotten some of these words out by looking down, by studying the button on his starched white shirt, but now she looked into his eyes again. He was staring at the black shadows behind the barnboard refreshment shed, and a muscle in his jaw clenched and jerked. Anne rested a loving fingertip on that taut muscle. Con pulled back from her. The embrace that had been so secure and safe turned tight and angry.

"Con?" she whispered, frightened.

"I don't want to get into it," he said flatly.

"Con, you *are* in it."

He tried to keep dancing, but Anne was no longer moving. "Is this the time and place?" he demanded. "What is your problem, Anne?"

"It's our problem," she hissed. "And the problem is, I'm pregnant."

He tried to cut her off before she said the word *pregnant*, but failed. "Anne, I'm not in the mood."

"You think *I'm* in the mood?" she snapped. "You think pregnancy is a *mood*? Well, it's not. It's the direct result of our — "

"Shut up," Con said.

Anne froze. I need you and you tell me to shut up? Kip, it was true; all the terrible things I said to you were true.

Anne was stiff with panic. Con began dancing again, and he shifted her on the floor, rather like a mannequin instead of a real person.

That's what I am, though, Anne thought. A mannequin. A store dummy. God knows I have the wardrobe, and the same amount of brains.

She began to cry.

Con hissed, "Not here. I cannot *stand* it,

Anne. Do you follow me? Read my lips." He made each word into a single sentence, spat from between his teeth like something vile. "I. Can't. Stand. It!"

Anne could not speak. Fears flew through her mind like a flock of blackbirds. I did everything wrong. I spoke wrong, I played the game wrong, I blew it completely.

She felt slack and limp, like an old clothesline sagging in the backyard. And then she thought, Why is it *my* responsibility to get everything right? Why isn't some of this Con's responsibility?

Con had danced her away from everybody, off the dance floor entirely, and back to the wooden bench where they had sat with Gary and Beth Rose. Beth Rose, let me tell you something about men, Anne thought. Let me tell you what happens when it's time to pay the price.

Con started to say something. His eyes fixed not on her eyes, but on the tear tracks that had worked down her cheeks to the fine slender line on her chin. They stared at each other. For a moment she thought he would touch the tears, and wipe them away, and they would hug in love and desperation and it would all be better.

But Con walked away.

She knew without looking that he was not asking a junior high girl in a Victorian maid costume for another soda, that he was not bringing the photographer to the wooden bench, that he was not rounding up his buddies so they could have a private party.

He was leaving.

For good.

Con transferred school so often that transferring Monday morning would be nothing for him. He wouldn't even have to move to do it; just saunter into his previous high school, grin at the vice principal, pass through guidance with a cocky salute, and enroll himself back where he'd been half of tenth grade. She knew Con. And his mother would sign the papers without even questioning what she was signing.

Oh, he was well named.

A true con artist.

And how I fell for him, she thought.

Chapter 14

Beth and Gary were dancing slow. He circled, shifting his weight more than dancing, and gradually Beth was swung into a different position and she could see Con and Anne behind her. They couldn't hear a thing because the band played so loudly. I can lip read, she thought, laughing to herself.

"Con, say something," came from Anne, and some emotion made her purse her lips more than usual, so that the words were as clear as written letters. "Con, I'm pregnant. It's our baby. You and me. *What are we going to do?*"

Beth nearly fainted. Not for a moment had she given Molly's rumor any credence. Molly was horrid; anything she said was lies; Anne was perfect. Blood rushed from Beth's head and she sagged against Gary more than dancers do. Gary simply moved closer to her, supporting her more.

She could still see Anne clearly. Anguish crossed Anne's face, and tears shone like jewels in the half light of the dance floor.

Beth Rose, who knew little, knew that Con would hate a public display. Although it meant she had to detach herself from Gary, Beth Rose straightened so she would have a better view of Con's face.

Blank as a piece of typing paper.

Does he really feel nothing? Beth thought. Or does it take all his self-control to hide what he does feel? Anne is crazy, bringing it up now. Why did she come to the dance at all? Why didn't she tell him before, or after?

"What's the matter with you?" Gary asked.

She had forgotten to continue dancing, but had come to a full stop to stare at Con, as if watching a freak show at the circus. Flushed, Beth mumbled that she had something in her shoe. Gary looked skeptical. She bent over to take off her shoe — and she was not wearing them. Like half the girls there, she had kicked her shoes off under the benches and was dancing barefoot.

"Pebble on the floor," Beth said desperately.

"Uh huh," Gary returned dryly.

Beth did not know what to say next. I haven't had enough practice, she thought. I haven't been around boys enough. Oh, if I were anybody else in this room I'd know what to say next.

She gave him a silly little smile, which she knew made her look like somebody cringing before the dentist's drill. They stood still. "Well, I'm really in a dancing mood, Beth," said Gary. He smiled at her. A sweet smile. Her heart flipped again. She started to say, "Me, too,

Gary," but he said first, "So maybe I'll dance with Jennie; she's sitting this one out." He smiled again. Identical smile. Beth found herself reflecting the smile, as if she were his mirror.

He's going to leave me here, right out on the floor in front of everybody, she thought. She wanted to throw up, or cling to him, but there were too many witnesses.

And then he was gone.

Like the sun behind a cloud.

Beth stood very still, trying to look as if she enjoyed standing alone, as if Gary had gone on an errand of her choice.

Gary bent over Jennie, and Jennie giggled, and looked around for her date. It was Bob, and Bob was laughing and nodding, because he was talking with another boy and didn't feel like dancing. Jennie took Gary's hand and in a moment they were dancing, just as she and Gary had been.

I'll pretend to myself that Gary is coming back any moment, and that'll make me feel okay. I can carry it off if I pretend to myself as well.

Chin high, skirt rustling, Beth moved toward the side of the room. Wallflower, she accused herself. You're not retreating, you're running. Whatever you call it, you're not sticking it out. A real woman would have gone over there and asked Bob to dance.

She shuddered at the mere thought.

On the wooden bench she had just left sat Anne Stephens.

Alone.

Frozen. Even her tears seemed frozen.

How absorbed I am by my own troubles, Beth thought guiltily. I actually forgot about Anne's. Beth looked around for Con, but did not see him. *No. He couldn't have.*

Timidly she sat next to Anne. She could still feel the warmth from when Con had been sitting there. "Can I help?" she said hesitantly.

Anne's head turned as if her neck hurt. "Nobody can help," she said tonelessly. "I have to go home alone."

"Hey!" said Christopher Vann. "You!"

The lead guitarist looked over at Chris, didn't like what he saw, and kept on playing. Christopher Vann did not appear to notice that the band was in the middle of a piece and three hundred people were dancing to it.

"Hey, stop it," Christopher said loudly. Loud enough to be heard over the boom of the guitars and the throbbing of the drums.

The guitarist was a fairly small man. He didn't much care for the way this drunken football player type loomed over him. Uneasily he said between verses, "Hey, buddy, buzz off, huh?"

"Who you telling to buzz off?" demanded Christopher.

The band could not draw any closer together. Their positions were fixed by their instruments. The keyboardist could not leave his keyboard and the drummer could not leave his drums. The guitarists could shift only as far as their electric cords would let them.

Both guitar players moved back into the collection of drums and cymbals. They were not on a stage. Kip had tried to rig one, but had had trouble with electrical outlets and given up. So Christopher towered over them and on top of them.

"Listen!" said Christopher. "I don't like the junk you're playing."

They finished the song they'd been doing. People clapped for the dance and stood waiting for the next one; the band was just back from a fifteen minute break. Now the kids wanted their money's worth.

"So what kind of junk do you like?" said the guitar player, smiling. "We aim to please."

Christopher lurched forward, stumbling over a cord. The guitarist put out a hand to steady Christopher, and Christopher threw the hand aside. Wonderful, thought the musician. Just what I need . . . some drunk slob who's going to smash my instrument. Guy looks older than high school. Who is he, anyway?

The musician scanned the crowd for help, but nobody had noticed anything yet. By the time they noticed, he would probably have a bloody nose and a broken guitar.

"I like hard stuff," said the drunk. He began listing bands whose specialties were obscenity and violence. They could never use that kind of thing at a high school dance. They'd never get another job again. Besides, the girl who organized the dance — Kip somebody — made it clear that one rule broken and the dance would be shut down like a nuclear plant with a leak.

The guitar player kept a friendly smile on his face, but he knew he looked like someone afraid of dogs smiling at a slavering rabid Doberman pinscher. The smile was a smirk of fear.

Caitlin said, "Watch me."

Sue shivered with delight and apprehension. Caitlin had nerves of steel. Sure enough, Caitlin led her foursome over to Molly. Molly was talking with a half dozen seniors, the kind that Con and Anne would be when they were seniors — special.

Caitlin interrupted everybody's conversation. They all let her, neither frowning nor continuing. Sue had read somewhere this was a sign of power — being able to interrupt at will. She waited for Caitlin's power display. Caitlin said without preliminaries, "So, Molly. Got your Harvard weekend all lined up?"

Jimmy began edging away. He didn't go in for this.

Molly, sensing a trap, smiled without committing herself.

Caitlin said to the seniors, "Molly brought a Harvard man. Or at least, a *former* Harvard man."

"What do you mean by that?" Molly cried.

"Yeah, we saw him lurching around," said one of the seniors.

"I mean he got kicked out, of course," Caitlin said to Molly. "Why else would he be at a high school dance? In November? When even colleges aren't on vacation?"

"He has a long weekend," Molly said stiffly.

"A hell of a long weekend," Jimmy said, pitching in when Sue pinched his arm.

Everybody laughed. Sue said, "It was so clever of you bringing him here, Molly. He can't get liquor here, so eventually he'll dry out on soda. Only you would think of that."

The senior girls began laughing. "Miaow," said one of them, turning away. "Listen, you juniors go have your fights on your own time, okay? We're busy."

"Okay," said Caitlin cheerfully. "Want to stick with us, Molly, and be juniors together?"

"I think I'm glad I'm graduating," observed a senior girl.

Sue and Caitlin linked arms with their boyfriends and moved away, laughing.

Christopher was making quite a scene, but because he was on the same floor level as the musicians, only the dancers pressed right up against the instruments realized it. Two senior boys, Billy and Roy, were mildly interested. "I remember him," said Billy. "Always picking a fight."

"Yeah," Roy said. "They threw him off the football team for fighting. You have to be some fighter for that to happen."

"How did he ever get into Harvard to start with?" asked Roy's date, Megan. Megan had a high-pitched voice, and it carried. It carried, unfortunately, as far as Christopher. Christopher swung around to listen, but Roy didn't notice. With a grin he said to Megan, "Must've lied on the application."

The second guitar player took one look at Christopher's face and quietly unplugged his guitar, preparing to beat a hasty retreat. The drummer thought exclusively of the dollars invested in his outfit and hoped that Billy and Roy were stronger than they looked. The keyboard man wondered if his accident insurance covered football players falling backward into his instrument.

As for Billy and Roy, they had time to remember that Christopher had been such a good sports player because he moved so fast, and then they were both bleeding.

Christopher would have landed a second punch on each of them, but he was having difficulty getting his balance back. There were plenty of witnesses now, but they were so completely surprised to have a fight break out next to them that they reacted even more slowly than Christopher.

One of them was Roddy.

Roddy had spent the entire week retreating. Retreating from Molly and her laughing at him.

Retreating from his mother and her conviction that Roddy was still dating Molly.

Retreating from Kip when she turned out not to be very nice after all. (He still couldn't understand that; he'd gone out of his way to be easygoing. He would never understand that to Kip, he was just being wimpy.)

And now everybody was retreating from Christopher Vann. Chris would win by default because all his possible opponents were just backing off.

On the other hand, Roddy did not have the personality for assault, especially when Christopher outweighed him by fifty pounds at least.

Billy and Roy struggled to get out of the way and into position to hit back. The girls screamed, especially Megan in her high, piercing voice. No music covered the screams. People began moving toward the noise, to see what was happening, so that within seconds there was a crowd, not just dancers.

Christopher regained his balance, drew his arm back and got ready to punch Billy. Billy, half on his feet, was nicely lined up to get his nose broken.

Roddy picked up the electrical cord that had been connected to the second guitarist's instrument, jerked it hard in front of Christopher, and tripped him flat.

The most amazing event of Roddy's life was not tripping Chris — it was that not one single person saw the electrical cord. What they saw was his bunched-up fist jerking through the air. Every person standing there thought Roddy had slugged Christopher and brought him down easy as that.

"Way to go!" yelled two of the witnesses, joyfully pounding Roddy's back and then less kindly pounding Christopher, who was down now and not likely to get up again.

"Oh, Roddy!" cried Megan, her voice carrying all the way to the rose arbor, "that was wonderful of you!"

Roddy began to laugh.

"Oh, Roddy, I adore you!" cried Megan.

Billy and Roy got up sheepishly and said thank you and shook his hand. Somebody had a real handkerchief, which Billy put to his nose, and Megan gave Roy a wad of Kleenex, which he pressed to his split lip.

"Quick thinking, Rod," said Gary, nodding congratulations.

Kip, of course, had planned for every possible event, and had hired two off-duty policemen. The two cops shouldered their way through the yelling teenagers. "All right, all right. So what happened?"

It was a woman cop. Roddy thought, she's not even as big as I am. What can she do with an ape like Christopher?

And then he thought, She could arrest *me* for starting it!

But the first version came from the shrinking guitarist, and the second came from Megan, and the third from the drummer. The police officer said sharply to Christopher, "Get up, young man, and explain yourself."

Christopher looked up at her, mumbled under the piercing threat of her glare, and got to his feet without help from anybody standing there. He didn't look sober, but he didn't look drunk, either. He looked totally humiliated and ready to be sick. The police officer withered him just by looking at him.

"You two boys all right?" she asked Billy and Roy. The boys nodded with embarrassment. Megan made little cooing noises over Roy's bloody lip and Roy obviously was praying that she would stop making such a big deal of this, but Megan didn't catch on and just got louder.

"Okay," said the policewoman very very loudly. "Okay, kids, listen up. Who came with this jerk? Somebody's gotta drive him home."

Molly was almost at the exit. She had change, she could call her parents to come for her. Better never to walk back in there than — but Sue and Caitlin yelled at the top of their lungs, "Hey, Molly! He's down this way! Over here! Want us to show you?"

The parents at the rose arbor smiled sympathetically at Molly. "Can you handle him, dear, or should we tell the police officer to take him home herself?"

Molly gritted her teeth. "I can handle him," she said, walking back through the cafeteria. Somebody — probably Kip — had flung on all the lights, and now the romance was ruined: You could see the dingy acoustical tile on the ceiling and the stainless steel counters where the lunch ladies served every day.

"Revenge," said Sue. "It's sweet."

"Probably even sweeter for Roddy," said Caitlin. "I hear Molly dumped him to bring Christopher in the first place."

"I can't believe Roddy was the one to hit him," Sue said. "It just goes to show, you can't judge by appearance. I'm going to give Roddy another chance. He's not such a geek after all."

"He can't be. He came with Kip."

"With *Kip? Really?*"

Caitlin nodded. "I saw them come in together."

"Amazing."

Molly reached Christopher. Sue and Caitlin weren't near enough to be able to watch. But they stationed themselves by the door to enjoy the final exit.

As for Roddy, he was grinning from ear to ear. He wished he had something else to do, like chew tobacco, or swivel a pair of drumsticks between his casual fingers. But Megan telling everybody how wonderful he was filled the gap. It occurred to Roddy that he could date Megan very easily right now.

He made a point of smiling at Molly when she rounded Christopher up. She did not smile back.

Roddy thought, May as well stick around. There might be some more action. Who knows what could happen next?

He grinned even wider.

Chapter 15

Kip missed the fight.

Moments before it broke out, the doorman came up to her. He was completely soaked. "Oh, you poor thing," said Kip. "But you still look impressive. In a wet sort of way."

He didn't laugh back. "Miss Elliott, I've got to get out of these clothes. I kept thinking the rain would stop and I'd dry out, but I'm soaked through. I'm gonna get pneumonia and I had that last winter. I know I promised you all night long, but I'm going to have to leave. I'm real sorry."

"Of course you should go home," Kip said. "Don't worry about it. Everybody had that great uniform on the way into the dance and they don't need it going out. Thank you for lasting this long. You were a wonderful addition to the dance."

He was pleased to be complimented. "You don't have to pay me for the rest of the evening," he told her.

Kip shook her head. "You earned it all."

They shook hands and she walked with him to the front exit. It was still pouring. "Good-bye," she said, "and thanks again."

The doorman nodded and dashed out into the rain.

Wind flicked into Kip's face. She stepped back into the foyer, and right onto somebody's foot. She was wearing tiny sharp heels and they came down hard.

"Ouch!"

Kip whirled around. "I'm so sorry, Con! I didn't know anybody was there!"

He smiled at her. It wasn't much of a smile. He was pretty annoyed to have been stepped on. "It's okay," he said. He moved around her and stood for a moment in the door, assessing the rain.

"Have to get something out of the car?" she asked. "Here. Use the umbrella." She picked up the enormous black umbrella she'd gotten for the doorman.

"No, thanks." Con looked neither at her nor at the umbrella. He walked out into the rain. He didn't run, the way the doorman had. He just walked. Within moments his hair was plastered to his skull. He didn't seem to notice at all. He got to his car, unlocked it, and sat for a while in the driver's seat.

Kip could not take her eyes off him. No, Con, no, she thought. Don't drive away. Anne needs you. Don't let her be right!

Con drove away. Alone. He vanished in the black rain.

Oh, Anne! Kip thought, her own heart hurting as much as Anne's must be right now. You were right. He is walking out on you.

The unfairness of the world hit her. She moved limply back into the foyer and leaned on one of the huge dividing pillars.

"You jerk!" came a furious girl's voice. "You stupid worthless jerk! What made you do that! You've ruined my whole evening. I *hate* you. Why did I ever come with you?"

Molly and Christopher were next to her in seconds. They never even saw her. Molly was pulling a raincoat over her shoulders and peering out into the rain. Deciding that her hair mattered more than her dress, she tugged the coat off and draped it over her head.

Christopher just stood there dully.

Molly began swearing at him. He roused himself enough to swear back but he lost interest after a few syllables. "Give me your car keys, you drunken idiot," Molly said. "Kicked out of Harvard. Who needs *you?*"

"Maybe I was," said Christopher. "But still...." He couldn't seem to figure out how to finish his sentence. Molly fished in his pockets to find his keys and saw Kip. "What's the matter, Kip?" said Molly viciously. "You don't have anything better to do than stand around and gloat?"

Gloat? Kip thought.

Molly grabbed Christopher's arm and hauled him out into the rain.

Wow, Kip thought. What did I miss?

She hurried back to the cafeteria and spotted Pammy, a sure informant. "So what happened with Molly and Christopher?" Kip asked.

Pammy giggled. "You missed that? Probably just as well. You would have been a wreck worrying that your dance was ruined. Christopher beat up Billy and Roy, and Roddy punched Christopher back, and the cops made Molly take Christopher home."

"Roddy punched Christopher back?" Kip said. "Did anybody have a video tape going? *That* would be worth seeing. What else did I miss? This will teach me to escort wet doormen to their cars."

"Let's see. Rumor has it that Con dumped Anne because she's pregnant. Nobody believes that because Molly started the rumor just to be rotten. Molly racks up boys like charges on her American Express card. Maybe this will slow her down a little." Pammy looked hopeful. Then, being Pammy, she changed the subject so fast Kip got confused. "All those hot little cheese things are gone. They were yummy. We went back for the little bacon things, too, and they're gone. Next dance be sure to order more of them, okay, Kip?"

"Sure," said Kip. But she gave no thought to bacon things, or cheese things, or even Molly. *Rumor has it. Molly started it.* Somebody *did* walk in on us in the bathroom. And now I have five hundred people here talking about Con leaving — and he just left. Pammy missed that. Must have been busy watching the fight with Roddy and Christopher. But Anne didn't miss it. She knows Con is gone. Poor Anne! I'd better go see if I can help her.

Sue dragged Jimmy to the other end of the cafeteria to join Anne and Con. "I don't want to go there," objected Jimmy. "What if it's true? I can't handle it."

"If it's true, we won't have to handle it," Sue said. "Anne will be the one handling it. Pick up your feet, Jimmy."

"I want to go real slow," Jimmy said. "I don't want to have to watch Anne handling it, either."

"Coward," Sue said.

"Runs in the family," said Jimmy.

Sue pulled him through the crowd. "Don't worry about it," she said. "Have faith in the Couple of the Year."

On a wooden bench in the farthest corner they saw the pink and ivory-gray gown that was Beth Rose. Thirty or forty feet away, Gary was dancing with Jennie. Sue dragged Jimmy farther on. Beth Rose and Anne were the only ones on the bench.

No Con.

Sue's eyes flew around the room.

But now they were close enough to see Anne's face. Stunned, totally wiped out, Anne was a shadow of herself.

It *was* true, Sue thought. The knowledge hit her as hard the second time as it had the first. She walked over to Anne. Jimmy read her face as well as Sue had, and he dropped behind, busying himself at the food.

Sue plunged right in. "Anne, I just heard. Are you okay?"

Anne's dull eyes focused on her. "Heard what?"

Oh boy that was stupid, Sue thought. Of course Anne doesn't know the whole room is talking about it. And if she finds that out from me I'd rather be dead. What I have to do is get her out of here before she realizes the gossip is spreading like that lightning. "That you weren't feeling well," she said quickly, trying to cover up.

Anne looked away. "I feel lousy."

"Want us to drive you home?" Sue asked.

Anne got straight A's. She was no fool. If Sue was offering a ride home, it could only be because Sue knew that Con wasn't around to take her himself.

Home, Anne thought. The minute I walk in early without Con I have to tell my mother and my grandmother. "No, thanks," she told Sue.

Sue looked at Beth Rose. Beth did not look anywhere but at the floor. She was good at watching the floor; she did it all the time under normal circumstances.

Sue knelt down in front of Anne, feeling both stupid and yet right. Taking a limp hand in hers she said softly, "I'm sorry, Annie. I'll help you if you'll let me."

Anne trembled. Her eyes locked with Sue's. Sue thought that Anne would break down, and she didn't know if that was the right thing or not.

But Jimmy couldn't stand the emotional level the girls were reaching. "Oh, big deal," he said. "So they've split up. Happens all the time. Anne's tough. She doesn't need Con."

Everybody looked at Anne. She didn't look tough. She looked as if she needed Con desperately.

The band started a very fast, very wild number, with hard crashing chords and zinging guitar slides that hurt the ears. Out on the dance floor the kids burst into crazed stomping and flinging of arms and legs. Gary led the way.

Anne laughed, and it sounded like a bell with a crack in it. "That's one point of view," she said to Jimmy. "A person can make it on her own, right?"

"Right," Jimmy said.

Anne stood up. "Come on, Beth!" she cried. "We're both alone. We'll dance together. Who needs boys?" She grabbed Beth's hand and dragged her out among the dancers.

They swirled in spinning, uneven circles, jerking heads and spines, thrusting out toes and wrists. Like a whirlpool in a high tide, Beth was swept into the dance, spun around by it, past Anne, away from Sue and Jimmy, between Gary and Jennie, up to Bob, Jennie's boyfriend.

It was like the *Twilight Zone*. The cafeteria no longer seemed romantic, but just poorly lit. She did not seem to be dancing herself, but thrown about by some greater force. Beth Rose wanted to scream, but the music screamed for her, vibrating across the room, piercing her ears, making her dance with more and more violence.

Anne was terrified. Where her strength had come from she had no idea. She did not know what emotion she was experiencing. Not anger. Not fear. Something dreadful: cold and hot, frantic and panicky.

Like the edge of a cliff, tempting her to jump.

It was ten-seventeen.

Gary, dancing with Jennie, was oblivious to the world.

Anne, madly dancing alone, was caught in the cyclone of her own fears.

Emily was leaving the emergency room, standing in the bathroom with the nurse, using the nurse's lipstick and powder. Matt was hanging in the doorway, telling her to hurry up. Her father was standing behind Matt, telling her to slow down.

Beth could not bear the crazed energy that had seized them all. Suddenly she yearned to be alone — *had* to be alone. She fled behind the scarecrow to the corner where she had hoped Gary would kiss her, and there in the shadows she leaned against the wall and shivered.

Kip, seeing Anne dance alone, decided that she, too, could dance. She didn't need a boy, either. What was this but a time for dancing? A time to forget your troubles and lose yourself in the satisfying repetition of rhythm and footwork.

Separated by the smallest of distances, their hearts and their minds were worlds apart.

Outside, the storm began to wind down. The wind lessened. The rain stopped completely. The center of the storm shifted. Now the lightning was on the horizon. The thunder came many seconds later, a faint echo instead of a jarring boom.

One last gust tore across the open playing fields and the wide parking lots. An old maple tree, whose core was eaten away by age and disease, began to split. A huge weakened limb tore from the tree. Thousands of tiny branches and twigs brushed the air. The roots and bark of the dying tree screamed in protest.

Halfway down, it caught the wires that brought electricity into Westerly Senior High.

Without fanfare, without warning, the lights went off inside the decorated cafeteria.

The instruments were instantly silenced.

The dancing ceased.

The dark came down, frightening, total darkness, enveloping everyone.

Chapter 16

This is my life, Anne thought. The lights are out. And they're not going to come on again, either.

The strange energy that had tossed her into the dance abandoned her. She felt as weak as if she had just been through some terrible illness. She could hardly stand, let alone dance.

For several moments the room was eerily silent. Then the chatter, the giggling, the shouting began. "Where are you?" a girl screamed, making the most of anonymity. "I'm over here," bellowed a boy.

"Ooooooh, I just touched something slimy!" Megan screamed in her high voice.

"Ooooooh, I just touched something sexy," said a boy very clearly. The whole room dissolved into laughter.

Shuffling feet replaced the scuffling sounds of the drummer. Outstretched hands found the wrong places or the wrong people, and laughter rocketed around the room.

Anne tried to orient herself. She had been

near the far wall. If she backed up she'd be at the food barn. Behind that would be the wall. She yearned for the wall. Solid. Safe.

She began inching toward it. She had never been afraid of the dark, and yet she felt things coming out of it, trying to hit her, and she cringed as she moved.

The junior high kids who were supposed to be waiters and waitresses were giggling like maniacs. Drinking soda in the dark, they began throwing cheese balls at each other and squashing them under their feet.

Anne found the wall. She felt it, her arms outstretched to their greatest length. Nobody else, and no objects, shared her wall. She walked her fingers up the wall. Nobody. Nothing.

Am I still sane? she thought.

Twice people literally passed over her. Feeling their way along the wall, they were headed for the pay phones in the front foyer. A girl tripped over Anne's foot. "Oooof. Are you okay?"

"Yes," said Anne. She was weeping. Her face and throat were soaked as if she had been in the rain. The couple passed on over her, like any obstacle to a journey, and bumped into somebody else.

"Oooh, who's that?" the girl squealed.

"Amanda and Jason."

The four talked about the blackout, how long it might last, and whether they should go home. "I just heard some hot gossip," Amanda said.

"Yeah? Tell all. I love even cold gossip."

"Anne Stephens is pregnant and Con walked out on her."

"That's not hot. I heard that half an hour ago."

No, Anne thought. No, no, no, no. Kip, whom I trusted completely. Kip told? Let it not be true. Not Kip!

But it was true. Their conversation drifted back to her. Well, I can't pretend now, Anne thought. The whole school knows. No matter what I decide, no matter whether Con's around or not, it's out.

It's not just my mother and grandmother I have to face.

It's my whole world.

It's every class, every kid, every teacher, every parent.

Kip had told.

I might as well lie down and die, Anne thought, but she did neither. She wept. When the lights come on, I will look so awful. But who cares? You can't get any lower than I already am. It can't get worse.

Beth Rose was close enough to embrace the scarecrow. He's my partner, she thought crazily. I could dance with him in the dark. Or even in the light. And who would know the difference? There's old Beth Rose Chapman, they'll say. Dating a scarecrow again. Just her type.

Now the rest were over the initial fear and enjoying the sudden complete dark! They were treating it like some special effect arranged by Kip for their entertainment.

"Gary?" she said. "Gary, where are you?"

She spoke too softly for anyone to hear, let alone Gary, who must be on the far side of the room. She didn't really want him to hear. How would it make her feel better when he discovered how desperate she was? How frantic she was for rescue?

Rescue. But I'm not afraid of the dark. I kind of like the dark. I want him to rescue me from being unpopular.

But that, too, was a kind of darkness.

Beth Rose waited, hoping her guardian angel would guide Gary across the floor to her, but of course that was ridiculous. Gary would stay where it was fun: in the midst of Jennie and Bob and that crowd, laughing until the lights came on. For a person like Gary, Beth thought, the lights were always on.

Perhaps the blackout was a fortunate thing, though. She could make her exit in the dark and not have to look at any of them. She wouldn't have to leave with her head hung, in failure. She would just not be there when the electricity was returned to the cafeteria.

She worked her way around the walls, stepping over people when she felt them with her outstretched fingers, apologizing, responding to their giggles with her giggles. Eventually she reached the long black corridor.

Somebody stepped on her with a bone-crushing weight.

She could not stifle her moan of pain.

"Oh, I'm sorry. I'm so sorry. I didn't mean to do that. I knew I would do that." A boy's voice. Hands patted her anxiously, found her arms, pulled her back on her feet. "Are you okay? Did I break any bones? It sounded as crunchy as potato chips!"

"I'm fine." She did not recognize his voice. She hung onto him. "I think it was more my shoe and the hem of my dress."

"Oh, no. I probably ripped the whole dress."

"I hope not. But we'll find out when the lights come on."

The hall was so completely, utterly dark. People poured up and down, hunting for adventure. To judge by laughter and silly jokes, they were finding it.

"Which way are you going?" Beth asked the boy.

"I'm leaving. I'm having a lousy time."

"Don't go," she said.

She was shocked at her own voice. There was a desperation in it that she had not even known she was feeling. Misery. *Don't go*. It was a cry of anguish. Hold onto me in the dark. Please don't go away. Stay with me.

Hysterically laughing people, at least ten or twelve of them, stumbled past. Shrieks of, "I'm tripping on somebody's feet!" "I can't see where I'm going!" "Do you *believe* this?" "Wonder how long it'll be off." "Let's go outside and shine the car headlights on ourselves so we can see who we're kissing!"

Wild laughter.

Pounding feet.

Pushing bodies.

And then they were past. It was quiet in the

hall. The cafeteria doors closed with a slap.

Very slowly she put her fingers out.

Nobody else was there.

She swung her arm in a circle.

She touched nothing.

He left me, she thought. He didn't even know who I was, and he knew I was a loser.

The next group poured out of the cafeteria. "I guess there won't be a King and Queen of *this* dance," said the first voice. "You have to be able to see who you're voting for."

"I thought maybe Beth Rose and Gary would be it. They looked so wonderful."

"Yeah, but they didn't come together. She came alone. That's why he was with her. They were just the only two people who didn't have dates."

The voice and the body that owned it crawled over Beth at that very same moment.

No, Beth thought. No, no, no, no, don't let me hear that!

But she had heard it, and it was true.

Her dress was nothing. Her special aura didn't exist. Her personality had not changed. She was nothing more than the only girl there that Gary could bother with. And that was all.

It was a knowledge too terrible for tears. It lay on her like one of her mother's smirks. Oh Bethie, you can't do that. Oh Bethie, you're no good at that. Oh Bethie, nobody will think that's interesting. Oh Bethie, go back and try again, you've failed this time, too.

I am truly Cinderella, Beth Rose thought. The lights went out like the clock at the palace striking midnight. I'm no longer dancing with Prince Charming. My dress isn't magical and neither am I. The dress is just cloth and I'm just Beth Chapman.

She walked dully toward the phones, not worrying about hitting anything in the dark, just stumbling forward.

There would be no coach and four to take her home, either. Just a mother very annoyed because she had to stay up so late waiting.

Two of the junior high girls, leaping about in the dark in their long black maid skirts, bumped into the carefully stacked pumpkins. There was a clatter as heavy invisible pumpkins tumbled over each other and hit the floor. The boys, horsing around next to the girls, bent over to identify the strange sounds and felt split pumpkin on their fingers.

"All right!" shouted an eighth grader. "Let's have a pumpkin fight!"

Kip, across the cafeteria, screamed at the top of her lungs, "Don't you *dare* have a pumpkin fight!"

The kids paused momentarily. "What can she do to us?" pointed out a seventh grader. "She can't even find us."

"I've got a handful of wet disgusting pumpkin pulp!" yelled an eighth grade boy. "First person I catch I'm going to rub it in her hair."

"Sexist," shrieked one of the girls. "Rub it in a boy's hair."

"No fun in that," said the eighth grader, feeling his way over the fallen pumpkins.

His best friend began jumping up and down on the pumpkins to split the rest of them open.

Kip, shouting, "I'll kill you! You ruin my dance and I'll kill you!" came tearing across the room. She forgot about the wooden swing and ran into it full speed. There was a couple sitting happily making out in the dark and she landed right on top of the boy.

"Kip, give me a break," said the boy.

"How do you know it's me?" she said.

"You're the only one dumb enough to get involved in a junior high pumpkin fight instead of enjoying the dark," he told her. He helped her to her feet, but not from charity. It was because he wanted to get back to his girl friend.

Kip headed toward the squelching sounds. The junior high kids were screaming with delight. Kip began grabbing any arm she could feel. The first person cried, "Ouch! It wasn't me. I'm just standing here. I promise. I didn't throw any pumpkin!"

"Stand somewhere else then," said Kip.

She worked her way forward and found a definite culprit. He was slimy with pulp. Kip's fingers dug into his arms. "Gotcha."

"What are you going to do with me?" he said. "You don't even know who I am and you don't have any lights for detective work, either." He yanked free and she could hear his feet hitting the pumpkins. What a mess it would be, tracked all over the room!

"Here's a flashlight." A voice in the dark shone a light right in her eyes, blinding her. She felt past the glare and grabbed the handle.

"Where'd you get it?" she demanded. But she didn't wait for an answer, because she recognized the junior high boys. "Evan and Brock!" she screamed. "I'll kill you. I'll call the principal. I'll call your fathers."

"Come on," said Evan. "We'll clean up. Promise. Don't tell on us. Good clean fun."

Kip turned to her unknown benefactor. "Are there any more flashlights where this came from?"

"Custodian's closet. No, I checked. Just that. Some kid threw up in the bathroom and I went to find a mop."

"Oh yuck. You truly are a saint. Cleaning up that. I think I would draw the line."

"I would, too, except the kid was my brother. If he wasn't in the bathroom getting sick he'd be out here tossing pumpkin pulp."

"I know the type," said Kip. "I have four brothers of my own."

"I know. Your brother George is in my sister Kate's class."

Kip flashed the light all over him. "Who are you?" she said. He was certainly nice-looking, but not the least familiar.

"I'm a senior," he explained. "We moved here this summer. I wanted to murder my folks for making me miss my senior year back home. I'm not crazy about Westerly High, but it'll do."

"So you've been here — what? — eight weeks?"

"Including summer, four months. A long four months."

"I'm glad to know you," Kip said.

"You don't know me. I haven't told you my name. And if you don't stop blinding me with that flashlight I never will tell you my name."

Kip screamed at two more boys attempting to find pumpkin pulp to throw. "You ruin my dance and I'll ruin you!" she yelled. "I have four younger brothers and if there's one thing I do well, it's stomp on junior high boys. Line up over here, you lousy seventh graders! I'll finish you off. Don't be cowards. Line up."

The band leader came over to her. "You're easy to find. If not by flashlight, then by voice. Flash the light over here, will you? We need to get up all our cords. They're tripping people."

"We're going to be stuck here for hours," said the senior cheerfully. "I read it in my horoscope."

"You read horoscopes?" Kip said in disgust.

"Certainly. But only after I've read all the comics and Ann Landers. I suppose you do important things like read the articles."

"No, but I read the headlines. And I never look at horoscopes. They're trashy."

Being the one with the flashlight made Kip the source of all attention, the focus of all eyes. People wanted to see where they were, who was with them, what they crunched under their feet. Girls who had tucked their shoes under some bench wanted Kip to locate them. Chaperones wanted the rose arbor moved away from the door so it wasn't a safety hazard. Kip got people to do this by the simple technique of shining her light in the nearest eyes and saying, "*You!* Do that!"

Fifteen minutes passed before she remembered her flashlight friend. He was nice, she thought. And cute. I liked him a lot. And he admitted to me that he's lonely here. And of course, with all my feminine intuition I acted on it right away. Asked him to go out with me, sat and flirted with him. That guy I fell on top of was right. I *am* the only girl in the world who would break up a pumpkin fight instead of necking.

The battery in her flashlight died.

She was instantly anonymous.

The demands upon her instantly stopped.

If his sister Kate is in my brother George's class, I could telephone home and ask George. . . . George? Ridiculous. He'd never tell me anything. He'd make me pay. But then, it might be worth it.

Anne found her tears strangely strengthening.

What chemical property could tears have, lying there on her cheeks, that absorbed agony? How could sobs that wracked her chest become peace that lay on her heart?

Not peace, no. Calm was a better word. The volcanic explosion was gone, and the dreadful panic was gone, and even the grief. She felt that whatever was coming, she could handle.

For whom have I always been perfect? she thought. Not for Con. It wasn't Con I was so afraid of telling. It's my own family.

I've lost Con.

But you don't lose your mother. No matter

what you've done, your mother is there. And she'll love me still. She'll yell and sob and maybe throw something, and call Daddy up in Europe and he'll fly home and they'll all feel betrayed the way I feel betrayed by Kip and Con . . . but they'll love me still.

Time to go home. If I have to face the music alone, so be it.

Anne began feeling her way around the cafeteria toward the front lobby. It took less time than she expected. Kip's decorations and props were not against the wall, but arranged to make the huge room into small areas. She walked into the hall. It was filled with people placing bets on when the electricity would come back on.

The front foyer doors had been propped open. Altogether there were six huge doors, of which usually only two were used. Now all were open. The rain was over. Clouds had been blown away by the wind. An almost full moon gave a ghostly light to the steps and filtered slightly through the six doors.

There were three pay phones. Each was busy, and each had a line of people waiting to use it.

Anne walked out onto the steps in front.

The cold did not bother her. It iced her heart, making her strong (or possibly frozen) and she stood, waiting until the phones were free, so she could call her mother and put the whole dreadful sequence into action.

Chapter 17

"I've changed my mind," said Mr. Edmundson. "I'm not taking you kids to the dance. We're going home."

"Daddy!" Emily cried. "Daddy, come on. After all we sacrificed we deserve the dance."

"No. Your feet are bandaged, and there could be more wires down, and you'd endanger your lives a second time. We're driving home."

Emily burst into a flood of tears.

Never before had she seen proof of what a splendid weapon tears were. Her father was so alarmed he almost drove off the road. "Emily, really, I'm making the right choice," he said frantically.

"No, you're not," Matt said. "You should let us go. The storm's practically over. The town is crawling with utility company trucks. And now we're on the main highway, not a stupid back road like Mink Rock."

Emily, seeing the effect on her father, wailed more loudly. I never knew I was such a scheming woman, she thought. Matt squeezed her hand. "I know you're faking," he whispered in her ear. "I've seen real tears from you and your eyes are dry, woman. You can't con me."

Her father said, "Well. . . ."

"Daddy, please, please, please? It's only fair. And Matt's arguments are good."

"You didn't need to say that," Matt said. "It's redundant. Everything I say is reasonable and logical. He knows that."

"I don't know it," said Mr. Edmundson. "You're the lad who sent my daughter through a lightning storm among live wires."

"I didn't have anybody else to send."

"Nobody sent me. I went by myself. Daddy, stop turning. The high school is straight."

"You've missed half the dance, Emily."

"And that means half the dance is left," Matt told Emily's father. He turned to Emily. "How do you like that for mathematics? I guess I should be a computer wizard, and not a disc jockey. I mean, with a numbers skill like that I could take over the world. Lee Iacocca, move over."

"Lee Iacocca is in cars," said Mr. Edmundson.

"If that's not higher mathematics, I don't know what is," said Matt.

Mr. Edmundson frowned at the wet road ahead of him. "You know, Emily, this kid is pretty lippy."

"Isn't it fun?" Emily agreed.

They all began to laugh.

Matt said, "Concentrate on your driving, Mr. Edmundson. Emily and I have something to attend to."

"Okay."

Matt said, "Let's kiss."

"I can't kiss you in front of my father."

"Why not? He knows how it's done. Anyway, he's seen us before. Look what truck is ahead of us, Emily. It's the television station. Probably covering the storm. Let's flag them down and tell them what we did. I want to be a hero."

"You are a hero," Emily pointed out.

"They already know," said her father. "I telephoned them. They're headed for the high school to interview you. I was just giving them a chance to get there. This way you can make a grand entrance."

Emily and Matt twisted in their seat to stare at him.

"My daughter risks her life and you think I'm going to let it slide by as if it's nothing?" he said.

Emily began shivering.

"You cold?" Matt demanded. "What's the matter? Turn up the heat, Mr. Edmundson, she's cold. You cold, Emily?"

"I'm boiling. The vents are all pointed at me. I can't go on television. My hair is a mess. I'm wearing blue jeans. You can't go on television in blue jeans."

"Sure you can. President Carter did it all the time," Matt said. "Anything he could do, you can do."

"I'll throw up," Emily said. "I'll be so nervous I'll throw up on their feet."

"If you were going to throw up you'd have thrown up on Mink Rock Road," Matt said. "You're fine. You look lovely. You'll be the hit of the eleven-thirty local news."

"Especially if I throw up on their feet."

"Stop worrying about their feet," ordered Matt. "Worry about *your* feet. Here. Lean on me." He leaped out of the car in front of the high school steps and held the door for her.

Emily got out very carefully, and touched the ground as if touching china. But her feet were still anesthetized. She was standing without standing, or at least without feeling. "Emily," said her father, "get crafty. Lean on the boy."

They all laughed.

The television crew went on into the building to find the young people they were going to interview.

"Hurry up," said Mr. Edmundson. "You think my daughter went through all this just so you could be late for your television deadline, Matthew?"

"I'm going to like this family," Matt said. "You guys are all crazy. I like crazy people. No, I'm going back to my original idea. I'm going to be a disc jockey. Come on, Emily, we have to get in there and shine."

"I won't shine. I'll be awful. I'm not going. Daddy's right. We should go home."

"Nope," said Matt. "People who run through

lightning are also good on television. It's a known fact. Find it in any almanac. Pick up your feet, Emily. Or you want I should carry you?" He beamed at her, his big goofy smile crinkling his eyes and then fading back to normal.

"I want you should carry me," she said.

Mr. Edmundson said, "I think this relationship is progressing a little faster than Emily's mother and I had in mind."

"Happens in lightning storms," Matt told him. "Known fact."

It was while they were shifting the rose arbor that Kip's flashlight was momentarily shone down the hall to the foyer. The light lasted for only a second or two, and then turned back to the heavy barrel in which the white birch clump was planted. Several boys took hold, grunted, and moved it far to the left. They dismantled the arbor and moved the potted silk roses over by the birches. Now you could enter and leave the cafeteria without smashing into the arbor.

In the fraction of a moment that she had light, Beth Rose saw the drinking fountain ahead of her and decided to have a sip of cold water before she phoned her mother. In the same fraction of light, somebody behind her recognized the pink and gray of her gown.

"Beth?"

It was dark again. She turned and saw nothing but velvety black.

"Beth, it's Gary. Stand still. I'll catch up to you."

She stood still.

Very still.

Except for her heart.

It beat like the drums of a thousand troops.

It was too dark even to see his profile. The hall was surrounded by classrooms and these doors were locked, so they couldn't even open the classroom doors and get a glimmer of moonlight from those windows. Gary's fingertips located her shoulder, and crept slowly around her back until he had a hand on each shoulder. Beth said, "Hi, Gary."

"You all right?"

"The dark shook me up a little at first. Now I'm used to it."

"Were you on your way outdoors?"

"No. Going to the phone to call my mother to come pick me up." Why am I not saying something flirty? Why not pretend I was looking for him? Why did I have to remind him that I came alone, uninvited, and my mother has to drive me around instead of a boy who loves me?

Gary said, "I don't suppose the power will be off very long. They won't want five hundred kids stranded in the dark over here. The utility company will have trucks out by now." He talked about power outages he had known, blackouts the restaurant had suffered, and a brownout that had ruined a computer program of his.

You dummy, Beth thought. I don't care about electricity. Except whatever's between us. We're standing here in the dark and you're holding my shoulders? Get your act together,

Gary. Fall in with my fantasies. *Kiss me.*

Out loud she said, "You don't realize how important electricity is until you lose it."

The absurdity of her remarks compared to what she was feeling made her laugh. Beth tried to squelch the laughter because she didn't want to explain it, but to her horror she cried instead.

For some people tears and laughter are very close and for Beth Rose they were inseparable. Sometimes she could not even tell if she felt grief or joy, because her body reacted with the same tears and laughter no matter what.

"What's wrong?" Gary said in alarm.

Well, if *he* won't move his hands and put his arms around me, I'll move mine at least, she thought. I can't lose because it can't get worse. She put her arms around him and rested her head on his chest and sobbed.

Gary was horrified. "Beth," he said desperately. "Beth, don't cry."

"Okay," she said and stopped crying.

They stood there. "How could you stop crying so fast?" he asked. "It was like a faucet turned off."

"It *is* kind of like that. Some people cry for hours. I cry for fifteen seconds and then I'm fine. I read somewhere it's chemicals pouring through you. I guess mine pour very fast."

She could feel Gary laughing, his chest quivering beneath her cheek. He said, "But what was wrong? What made you cry at all?"

"The whole evening. It just built up."

"The whole evening?" he repeated. "I thought most of it was okay."

Okay. "Most of it was wonderful," she told him. "I was so scared of coming alone. I couldn't believe I was doing it. But I had to. It was the dress. I had no place else to wear it." *I'm saying this out loud?* she thought. *What is it about the dark that makes this like a confessional?*

"The dress," said Gary. His hands actually moved over the back of the dress rather than over Beth, as if trying to remember by touch, getting clues so he could remember this dress of hers.

Beth found herself telling him all about Aunt Madge's prom, and Virgil Hopkinson, and the dry cleaner's bag that had kept the dress dust-free all these years, and her mother's sarcastic remarks. Somehow this led to telling him about Con and Anne, and that brought her back to tears, but these lasted longer.

Gary said nothing.

She was not surprised. How was he supposed to make an intelligent remark after *that* outburst? "I'll never be able to face you in school again," she said. "I'll have to wear a mask in the halls. It's a good thing we don't have any classes together."

"What makes you say that?" Gary said. "I thought it was interesting hearing about your Aunt Madge, and when the lights come on I'll look at the dress again."

"You don't remember the dress?"

"Sort of. I remember you stood there looking really pretty and fragile and the roses were on one side and the pumpkins on the other, and I wanted to move away from the pumpkins and have you stand where you fit in."

Oh, Gary, she thought, the gifts you have given me tonight! I know I can be beautiful. I know I can be desirable. I know I can dance. I know I can be good company. What more can I ask?

Well, I *could* ask you to love me forever and take me out seven hundred days in a row, but you won't, and I'm going to love you, anyway. "Thank you for coming over to me," she said.

For several minutes they were quiet. People scuffed by in groups and patches. Bits of conversation floated by. ". . . repair truck in the parking lot." "Kip's in there throwing pumpkin around." ". . . most wonderful dance I've ever been to." ". . . pumpkin pulp in my hair, I'll kill him." "And now I have a crush on Stephen as well as a crush on Michael."

Gary said to her, "You were the only girl who came alone."

"The only one dumb enough."

"Brave enough," Gary corrected.

She shrugged, but he couldn't see this in the dark. His hands were no longer on her shoulders, so he didn't feel the shrug, either. After a while she realized Gary didn't know how to end their conversation. You've given me so much, it's only fair I should give you a way out, Beth thought sadly. "Let's work our way on down the hall, Gary. Then I can phone my mother."

"If you want to stay until the end of the dance, I'll give you a ride home," he said.

Her heart skipped beats. "Gary, you don't have to feel obligated to me."

"I don't feel obligated. I just said I'd be glad to give you a ride home, that's all."

"Thanks. I'd like that." She did not pretend that he'd kiss her good-night in her driveway; if he wasn't going to kiss her now in the dark when their arms were around each other, then he never would.

"Mind heading back to the cafeteria?" Gary said. "Kip may need some help in there if kids are having pumpkin fights."

Great, Beth thought. I get to wade in mashed pumpkin in this dress. Aunt Madge will love it.

And then she thought — but Aunt Madge *will* love it. She wanted the dress to have one more romantic adventure — and it has. I've had my first; the dress has had its second. And who could ask more of a Saturday night than that?

Christopher's steps became shorter, his lurching more pronounced. Molly was far too small and slim to support him, so she kicked his ankle instead, to shock him awake. Christopher looked at her in pain and astonishment, but he did navigate the stairs without falling.

When they reached his car, he put up something of a battle because he didn't want to sit on the passenger side. "You can't drive!" she spat at him. "I'm not going to get killed for your sake."

"I'm not drunk anymore. It wore off."

"Then why can't you walk and talk?"

"I'm tired. I haven't slept in days. Caught up to me."

Under her breath Molly called him all the names she knew. But they were standing very close, and no matter how softly she muttered, he heard them all.

"You lose, Molly," he said, words he knew would hurt her more than any mere insult.

Christopher felt a strange satisfaction in the night. Having failed at college, where everyone expected him to shine, he had come home and failed again publicly. It was more attention than he'd had all those months at Harvard, where consistently he was ordinary among the other stars. In some warped way, Christopher felt he had achieved something: The loss of respect of everybody at the dance was more of an accomplishment than anything else he could think of recently.

Christopher stared at the unfamiliar dashboard of the passenger side of his car. He tried to turn the radio on, but his radio didn't work unless the engine was going and Molly hadn't started the car.

She slid behind the wheel and eyed him with disgust. He was falling asleep with his mouth open, his hair flattened against the window, and the door handle pressing into his ribs. The lights in the parking lot suddenly went out. She was mildly startled, but it did not occur to her the entire dance was now in darkness. She simply started her engine and put on her headlights to see by.

So you think I'm a loser? she thought. *Never!*

Without nervousness she drove Christopher's unfamiliar car. Molly had never met the car she couldn't drive. Stepping hard on the gas, she hydroplaned over an immense puddle that was the result of blocked storm drains. Laughing to herself, Molly began to take corners very fast, letting the car do what it would. It soothed her to be in and out of control of the car; it was a reflection of her own soaring and falling evening.

She got on the highway, letting the speedometer climb way past the fifty-five limit. You had to say this for Christopher, his car had power. Shame he didn't match it. To humiliate her in front of the whole school, so that Sue and Caitlin and Kip and everybody else could throw it back in her face! I hate them all, she thought.

Knowing that they had won was too much for Molly. She could not stand it that Saturday night would end, and they would have a boy, and she would have a drunken jerk. She got off the highway, circled, and went in the opposite direction, headed back to Westerly High.

Anne saw the electric company trucks pull into the student parking area. She saw the huge cherry picker, and heard the chain saws buzzing, as the crews cut away the immense limb and the smaller branches and freed the electric cables. She saw the crowd of kids who stood in the drizzle watching, and the policeman who herded them away because of the danger.

None of it registered on her mind. She was simply cold.

Behind her the lights went on. The band began playing again. The kids began screaming again.

Anne stared at the crews. They wore thick gloves issued by the company that prevented current from going through them. She thought, If I were to go over and pick up the end of that cable and not have those gloves on, perhaps it would kill me. I could end it right now. Walk out there and die.

She tried to decide if dying would be easier than facing her mother and grandmother; if dying would be easier than knowing every day of her life — and every day of this baby's — than Con did not love her enough to stay. Blue with cold, unaware of it, Anne stood watching a live wire.

She did not notice the television crew, complete with cameras, strong lights, and microphones. She shifted out of their way from instinct, not recognition. She never saw the two kids in blue jeans at all.

In the foyer, the few kids who hadn't rushed back to dance again gasped when they realized the tv station was there. They raced after the crew, yelling, "Film me! Film me!"

Anne didn't race anywhere.

Oh, Con, she thought. *Con.*

Chapter 18

The moment the lights came on, Kip Elliott began circling the cafeteria. Think of me as a panther hunting her prey, she said to herself. I know my flashlight friend is out here somewhere.

But he wasn't.

She began to wonder just how well she had seen him behind the eerie shadows of the little flashlight. What if she didn't even recognize him when he turned up? But *he* knew *her* — surely he'd walk over when he saw her, to talk about their short adventure.

But he didn't.

I could call George right now, she thought. Ask him who this Kate is. Get a last name. But I know George. He hates girls. He probably won't admit that Kate exists. He'll tell me there's no Kate in the entire junior high and if there were he wouldn't speak to her, anyhow.

She scanned the crowd eagerly — and there was Roddy.

Their eyes met.

Oh, no, Kip thought. If I have the same puppy-wagging-its-tail-look that Roddy has, my flashlight friend will stay in the shadows and I'll never lay eyes on him again.

Roddy beamed at her.

She had no choice but to smile back. He bounced right over to her. "You were looking for me?" he asked happily.

After all the things she had said to him, he was forgiving her, and handing her the cue line she needed to make up for some of it. "Yes," said Kip. Her smile came easily now. "You were great, Roddy. I was the pits. I'm really sorry. I was in a foul mood and I took it out on you and I hope you can stand me after this. I missed the fight with Christopher, but everyone tells me you were fantastic."

"Oh, sure," said Roddy. "No problem. And I didn't do a thing with Christopher."

"Except knock him over. That's quite a lot, a football type like that. Don't be modest."

"Okay," said Roddy, willing not to be modest. "Listen, Kip, you've got pumpkin on your cheek."

Kip began to laugh. "Ah, romance. Thy name is pumpkin."

"What?" he said blankly. "Here. Here's a handkerchief." He handed her a nice clean folded square of cotton and she mopped her face while he watched intently. "No, farther over," he said. "Now you've got it."

"Maybe I should go to the girls' room and check." She thought she would check the halls for the flashlight friend while she was at it.

"No, no. You look fine now. They're starting another number. Come on, Kip, let's dance. We came together and we haven't even danced yet. Come on, Kip, let's dance, okay?"

"I'd love to," she said helplessly. Yet in a way, she meant it. Roddy was nothing to her, but he had brought her here. She had seen her own dance, and more importantly, seen herself. Some of it wasn't as nice as she expected, but she knew it was there now, and she could deal with it.

She danced with Roddy. He wasn't good. He twitched instead of dancing. But he was having a good time. In fact, thought Kip, filled with both surprise and envy, he was having a *great* time. What a wonderful attribute: to be able to have fun after such a rotten beginning.

I could learn from Roddy, she thought. I could learn to forgive and forget.

Occasionally they touched, but mostly they danced separately. Couples circled the floor, flushed with the excitement that comes from exhaustion, and change, and unexpected events.

The cafeteria doors swung open.

Two men with shoulder cameras marched in, and immensely powerful dazzling lights scored through the dancers. The kids broke apart and stared.

Television?

At their ordinary old school dance? There was nobody famous at their school, and nothing interesting was happening.

"Maybe it's the superintendent of schools," somebody said, "trying to show off how liberal he is to let us have a dance again."

"Maybe it's the mayor, showing how well he acts in a crisis, getting power back to his children stranded in the dark."

Kip's heart leaped. Could they possibly be covering her dance? Showing off what kids could do when they put their minds to it? But her decorations had all been moved! There was a pumpkin mess and no rose arbor and—

Everybody was pushing forward to see better. They became part of a crowd instead of couples. The band stopped playing. The cameras inexplicably turned away from the dancers and faced the doors.

In almost complete silence, they waited for some grand entrance.

"But it's nobody," Caitlin whispered, confused.

Some boy they'd never seen, wearing old clothes that didn't fit very well, and some girl who didn't look as if she had much to offer, either. The girl was laughing, and hanging onto the boy as if her feet hurt, not as if she loved him. She was wearing *jeans*.

"Jeans!" said Kip, honestly annoyed. Her formal dance? They were going to film some couple wearing jeans? If that isn't just like television! Featuring the one couple that's out of it, instead of the dozens who really represent Westerly High, she thought furiously.

The cameramen slowly followed the laughing couple inside.

"I know who that is," Jimmy said in astonishment. "That's Emily Edmundson."

"Never heard of her," said Sue.

Jimmy shrugged. "She's nobody. In my math class. I don't think she ever talks. She's just there."

"I never saw her before," Kip said. It irritated her that she could be totally ignorant of some kid in her grade who merited television coverage.

The teenagers were watching as if they were at home in front of the tube. It was even more mesmerizing to see a filming; they could not take their eyes off the demands of the cameras. Very very bright lights focused on Emily and her boyfriend. The crew motioned everybody else out of the way so that the reporter had a clear field.

"Her hair looks awful," Kip muttered to Beth Rose. "She could at least have gone to the hairdresser's if she's going to be on tv."

The reporter turned, and faced into the cameras, and smiled. Now they recognized him. "I remember those teeth," Gary said. "Those are eleven-thirty newscaster teeth."

Beth laughed. She never stayed up late enough to see those teeth. That's how you know you've led a boring life, she thought. When eleven-thirty is beyond imagining. It made her yawn to think of it.

"Tonight's fierce electrical storm," said the reporter in a very broadcasting sort of plummy voice, "caused more than annoying power shortages. In the western end of town, high winds brought down trees, and one of those trees caused a brutal car accident on Mink Rock Road. Very seriously injured was Jasper L. Chase, owner of the largest fuel company in the greater metropolitan area. He was a lucky man tonight, because the other car struck by this tree was driven by this young man, Matt O'Connor, whose passenger is this lovely young lady, Emily Edmundson. Matt and Emily left the safety of their car, crossing live electric wires and downed trees to reach Mr. Chase. While Matt performed lifesaving techniques, Emily ran through the lightning more than half a mile to telephone for help."

The reporter smiled and nodded, knowingly, proudly, as if in possession of secrets.

"We can't see Emily as she was," he boomed, "because Emily ruined her beautiful blue prom dress tearing it on branches; ruined the matching high heels, damaging her own bare feet, and ruined her perfect hairdo. You see, Emily and Matt were on their way to the first formal dance Westerly High has had in three years, and they paused to save the life of a stranger."

Another smile. Gary was right. They knew him by his teeth.

But we don't know Emily at all, Kip thought. Emily's in my history class, I remember that now. I've never spoken to her! She looks so nice. And kind of scared. She's looking at the microphone as if it could bite her. Emily! Enjoy yourself! It's your moment.

Kip would have loved to be in front of that mike, thinking of something clever to say. Especially with a boyfriend who looked like that. Once you got used to the crummy clothing, he was really something.

"Emily," said the reporter, holding the mike toward her, "how does it feel to be such a heroine?"

But nobody would ever know what Emily thought, because Gary Anthony performed his second rescue of the night. He didn't know it; it never crossed his mind that Emily was so embarrassed she was speechless, that she couldn't even think of a stupid thing to say, let alone something worth television coverage.

"All *right*!" yelled Gary at the top of his lungs. "Let's hear it for *Emily*!"

The entire room — five hundred kids — began clapping, whistling, shouting, and stomping for Emily.

Like packed cheerleaders, thought Emily, staring at them. She blushed so deeply she turned to Matt to hide her face. Matt loved every minute of it. "Wow," he whispered. "Do you have a lot of friends!" He took the mike from the reporter and said, "It was fun. Exciting. Not everybody gets to kick off a dance like that, right?"

"Right!" yelled the hundreds of kids back at him.

Matt abandoned the camera and the reporters and the lights, and even the mike. "But Emily and I came to dance!" he shouted. "Come on! You guys are practically ready to close up shop and we haven't had a dance yet! Let's have some music!"

He pulled Emily after him, and she followed, stumbling, because her feet were now beginning to get feeling back and none of the feelings were good. She made herself ignore the pain. Here was Matt thinking all these kids adored her! She had to live up to it. Or at least dance one dance.

Heroine.

The word took some getting used to.

But there was no time for Emily to get used to it. She and Matt danced: a wild rock number that used up a little of Matt's tremendous energy and totally sapped what was left of Emily's. She sank onto a bench and put her feet up on what looked like a rose arbor lying down. How strange.

Matt kept right on dancing in front of her, having a great time, not caring in the slightest that he no longer had a partner. Everybody kept coming up to Emily to tell her how terrific she was — how proud they were to know her!

Emily kept laughing.

This is impossible. I'm the one whose name they haven't been able to remember for sixteen years!

Sue and Jimmy. Gary and Beth Rose. Caitlin and somebody unknown. Pammy and Jason. Megan and Roy.

Will it last? thought Emily, laughing, talking with every kid she'd ever dreamed of being friends with. Will they be my friends on Monday? Tuesday? And ever after?

Or is it just tonight?

* * *

The lights came on when Gary and Beth Rose had gotten as far as the custodian's closet. Their eyes hadn't adjusted to the light when some kid half in, half out of the closet said, "Hey, Gary. Take this snow shovel, will you?"

"It's turned to snow out there?" Gary asked. "I didn't know it was *that* cold."

"No, it's pumpkin. The junior high kids had a pumpkin fight. I don't know what else to clean it up with."

Gary laughed. "I'm a great pumpkin shoveler from way back." He took the snow shovel and the other kid took a roll of paper towels and a can of spray cleaner. "I'll find you after we've cleaned it up," Gary said to Beth, smiling. He said nothing about the dress he had promised to notice when the lights came on, and his eyes weren't on the dress, anyhow; they were on the shovel.

Beth sighed.

Gary said, "I'm really sorry. I forget your name."

"Mike Robinson."

I thought he meant me, Beth thought, relieved.

"Yeah. Did Kip line you up for cleaning crew?" Gary asked.

"No. I was just there. The kids who are on clean-up brought blue jeans to change into. But I'm just wearing an old sports jacket and pants, anyway. No problem for me, they don't even have to be dry cleaned."

Fascinating, thought Beth. Intoxicating. Thrilling. My idea of romantic talk, too. Oh, well, it was nice of them to clean up for Kip.

The pumpkin really had created a hideous mess. Those junior high kids had had only five minutes, but they had been a very destructive five minutes. Beth Rose stood in awe of the ability to smash pumpkins in a hurry. The dance floor was now half as big, due to squashed pumpkin on the other half.

Kip didn't even look mad.

In fact, she was dancing, which seemed most unlike Kip. You would have expected her to be supervising.

The fact that Gary was going to drive her home gave Beth Rose a curious poise. Even though nobody else knew about it, she was able now to walk out onto the jammed dance floor and begin dancing alone. Jennie and Bob were on her right, Caitlin and her date, Sue and Jimmy, and all the rest.

When the electricity returned, people had wanted more light than before. There was no dim romantic atmosphere left. It was a real cafeteria now, with acoustical tiles hung with fishing wire and felt and mylar and satin leaves. Half the props and decorations had been shifted, or someone had fallen on them and broken something off. Beth would have expected Kip to be beside herself, but Kip didn't appear to have noticed anything wrong. She was dancing away like everybody else, lost in the beat and the music.

Sue stopped dancing so abruptly that both Beth Rose and Jimmy plowed right into her.

"Look at that!" she exclaimed, with such astonishment that they all whirled.

"Must be tyrannosaurus rex or something," said Jimmy, laughing at Sue.

It was a television crew.

Sue squealed with pleasure. "We'll be on the eleven-thirty news! Our first dance in three years! We're important enough for the news. Jimmy! How does my hair look?"

"Gotta be too late for the evening news," said Roddy.

"It's not. It's five of eleven. They'll make it if they hurry."

"Hurry?" said Gary skeptically. "They'll have to fly." He was leaning on his shovel, framed against the orange of the pumpkin remains. What a color shot it would make: handsome Gary in his tuxedo, the pumpkins strewn around his feet!

Beth walked over to him. "Let's be on tv," she said, smiling.

He grinned, put down the shovel, offered her his arm, and waltzed her toward the crew.

Chapter 19

The clouds were gone. Stars spangled the black sky. Anne stared at their patterns, looking for answers, finding none.

A car pulled very very slowly into the parking lot. A car she knew very well. She knew every ripple of the corduroy upholstery and every scratch on the crimson finish. Con's car.

At the foot of the steps, the car idled. She stood still. Con saw her. A full minute later he turned off the ignition, got out of the car, and slowly walked up the steps toward her. Anne looked at him. She was so drained of emotion that she felt none, looking at him, and no expression crossed her face because there was no feeling left in her heart.

"You don't have a coat on," Con said to her. "It's freezing out here. Why are you standing outside without your coat?"

She didn't answer. He pulled his own jacket off and draped it over her shoulders. She didn't react. "Are you waiting for your mother?" he said. "Did you call her?"

She shook her head.

"Well, stand inside. You're going to die of hypothermia." He walked her inside the school and the warmth hit her. Now she realized how cold she was. She looked at her hands: transparently blue, trembling. Con took them in his own and began to rub them. She watched the friction of their hands.

After a while Anne looked into his eyes, trying to see past the dark pools of iris into the mind that made Con drive back. His eyes told her nothing. She looked away.

Con drew a deep breath and stopped rubbing her hands. He simply pressed them between his own, as if they were both praying. "I'm sorry."

She nodded. "Me, too."

He couldn't seem to think of anything to add. He didn't touch her in his old way, either. He stood apart, and when he began rubbing the still-cold hands again, it was more like a medic with a stranger.

Inside the school, down the hall, they heard the music spring to life. Moments later the television crew rushed down the same hall, elbowing Anne and Con out of the way in their rush to get to the studio on time. Anne had never seen them to start with and barely saw them now. Con saw, but could not fathom what a tv crew could be doing at the school and forgot them the instant he looked back at Anne.

"I'm sorry," he said again.

"Once I broke a piece of my mother's wedding crystal, and I said 'I'm sorry' and she said 'Being sorry doesn't make the crystal whole.'"

Con swallowed. "Okay. Okay. You threw it at me so fast I couldn't think. I couldn't believe I had to handle that in front of everybody I've ever known. I just had to get out of there. I'm sorry, Anne. I really am."

Is he sorry he walked out of the dance? Sorry I told him so quickly? Sorry I'm pregnant? Sorry he has to get involved? Anne thought, I will have to interrogate him to know, and I don't have the strength.

Con had never seen Anne like this. Stunned. Cold inside as well as outside. "I'll drive you home, Anne," he said finally. "I don't — I don't want any part of this. I want it not to be. But — but okay. I'll go home with you. I'll be there when you tell your mother."

Anne looked at him again and narrowed her eyes trying to focus on him. But she couldn't see him clearly. She shivered.

"Okay," he said, drawing a deep breath. "Okay. *We'll* tell your mother."

She tilted her head slightly and the beginnings of a slight smile touched her lips. "You're pretty brave, fella."

"Yeah. That's me. Pure raw courage."

"I like that in a man."

"Let's go, then. Let's get it over with."

"No," said Anne Stephens. "I don't want to go. We've missed the whole dance. I want to go back to the dance."

It was Con's turn to freeze. "Anne," he said, dreading the sentence he had to speak, "they all know in there. There was gossip starting when I left. Molly started it. I guess she heard you telling Kip about it. There's not a person in the cafeteria that doesn't know."

Nothing could have amazed Con more than Anne's sudden happy smile. "Really? I thought it was *Kip*. I thought *Kip* told."

"No. Kip wouldn't do this to us. Molly started the rumor."

Anne's smile faded. "Oh, it's a rumor now?" she said in a hard voice.

Oh, Con thought, and we have her mother and grandmother to go. "No. It's not a rumor. You're pregnant and I walked away from it. Left you here alone." The muscle began twitching in his cheek again. He tried to relax, letting go of each muscle the way they learned in gym, but it didn't work. The muscle twitched involuntarily.

And after I face her family, I have to face mine, he thought. He knew what his mother and father would say. Con, we trusted you absolutely. We gave you freedom in which to be responsible. And look what you've done. . . .

Anne's chin lifted. "I don't care what everybody is thinking. We're going back in there and dance the last dance, Con. Together."

He would rather have fought a world war with his bare hands. Five hundred kids in there, all quoting Molly who described him — rightly — as the rat who abandoned Anne?

"Okay," he said. His stomach knotted like chicken wire. Calm down, he told himself. You're walking in together. She had to walk out of there alone. Con put his arm around her, feeling very shy, as if Anne were a woman he had never met. "You warm enough now?" he said, because temperature was a safe topic.

"I'm okay."

They walked toward the cafeteria door.

The muscle in his cheek throbbed until his jaw hurt.

Anne leaned on him.

Con seriously considered picking her up bodily and hauling her to the car. The car! "The car," he said happily, "is not in a real parking space. We have to go move it. And since we're moving it anyway, we might as well just drive on to your — "

"So we get a parking ticket. Big deal. What's a ticket at a time like this?"

"Right," said Con, who was having to take such deep breaths his own breathing winded him. My parents told me one more ticket and they'd ground me, he thought. That'll be the pits. I'm the father of this baby, I'm the rat who abandoned her, and I also don't have a car to drive.

He swung open the door to escort her in and it was the most difficult motion in his life. Walking away was a snap. Staying was pretty grim.

Everybody was dancing. Good. They'd be too busy to look up. Anne and Con could just slide along the wall, hopping over the apple barrels and the —

But they were not too busy to look up. Sue and Jimmy looked up, Bob and Jennie, Gary and Beth Rose, Kip and Roddy.

"You had to do this to me," Con said. "You had to give me an audience."

216

"I'm sorry. Bad timing. I couldn't help it. I was going insane and I split apart at the wrong moment."

"Next time tell me sooner."

"Next time?" she snorted. "If you think there's going to be a next time, you're out of your mind!"

He laughed. It was a real laugh, and so was Anne's. He kissed her, and it was a real kiss, and so was hers. "I love you, Anne," he whispered.

She began to cry.

"Oh, no, don't cry on me!" he begged.

"I'm not," she whispered back. "I'm really laughing."

"Then why are there tears running down your cheeks?" he murmured.

"You're fibbing," she said. "There aren't any."

He wiped them away with his right hand and held her chin lightly the way he often did before a kiss. "You're right," he said. "There aren't any."

They had gotten halfway across the room and reached the edge of the dancers. Con prayed the music wouldn't stop. He could not talk to a single person right now and that included Anne. The music was fast, which was bad, because he could hardly move, let alone dance fast.

"Wish it was a slow one," he mumbled to Anne. He was out of breath, as if they'd climbed into the cafeteria.

"So we'll dance slow." She leaned on him and they danced slow, paying no attention to the drums that whipped the rest along. He was glad they were the same height because her golden hair partially shielded his face, and when he saw kids looking at him, he simply moved her fractionally to the side, and her hair gave him privacy from the stares.

"First test," Anne said to him.

Con groaned. "Out of how many?"

"I don't know. I'm trying not to think that far ahead."

The music stopped.

Gary and Beth Rose walked over. Con felt panicky. Gary said, "You missed a good pumpkin fight, Con. I was the one who got to shovel it all up, ankle deep in pumpkin pulp."

"Kip give you a medal?" Con asked.

"No, but I got a pat on the back and that's something from Kip." Gary talked about the power blackout Con had missed. The tv crew, and Emily and Matt's rescue of the dying stranger. Con was able to look only at Gary, and not see the rest of the kids, and Anne was able to look only at Beth Rose.

The music began again and after that it was easier.

Beth Rose wondered if Gary knew how many gifts he had given that evening. Had he seen that he gave Emily a breather so she wouldn't have to talk into a terrifying microphone? Had he seen that he gave Beth herself a moment to cherish all her life — a moment of being utterly irresistible and beautiful? Had he planned to rescue Con from a whole room of curiosity seekers?

She had a sense that Gary was kind unawares. That he had a knack for doing nice things without noticing himself doing them. Perhaps that was the definition of charity: to do good without ordering yourself to do it.

"You keep doing this to me," Gary said.

"What?" Beth Rose asked.

"Just standing there in a daydream when I want to dance."

"I'm sorry."

"It doesn't matter. I'm used to it now. Doesn't throw me."

We're getting used to each other, she thought. Does that mean something? Do I dare read something into that?

Chapter 20

The last dance.

The band was exhausted. The long evening was over. Happy to be playing the final number, the musicians were grinning at each other, half performing, half packed to go.

The food was long since devoured.

The junior high waiters and waitresses abandoned the tables and found their own partners for the last dance. A few of them sported tell-tale patches of orange pumpkin pulp.

The clean-up crew, mostly freshmen and sophomores Kip had corralled by telling them it would look good on their records (an absolute lie: Records at Westerly mentioned only grades and test scores), were waiting by the exit. They were envious of the dancers and irritated by them, because they wanted to get the cleaning done so they could go home.

Kip and Roddy danced as if they had been partners all their lives. Roddy thought it was because Kip liked him now. Kip thought it was because Roddy mattered so little to her that it had become easy to be with him. But she smiled at him.

And there was her flashlight friend. Dancing by in the company of so many people that she could not tell which girl — if any — was with him. "Hi, there," he said to Kip.

"Flashlight," she said. "I never thanked you properly."

"I know. And I got Gary to shovel up the pumpkin for you and you never thanked me for that, either."

"If you'd introduce yourself properly, I could thank you properly," said Kip. She was shaking all over. Is this what falling in love is? The shakes? Then I've never fallen in love before because I've never trembled all over before.

"Mike Robinson," he said.

She stopped dancing with Roddy and shook Mike's hand. She liked his handshake. Firm without crunching. What would his kiss be like? What would it be like to have the name Kip Elliott Robinson? Would he have heart failure right now, this Mike Robinson, if he could read her thoughts? "Mike," she said, "welcome to Westerly High."

Roddy coughed slightly.

"And this is Roddy McDonald," Kip added. The boys nodded at each other. Kip fancied that Mike was sizing Roddy up to see what the competition was. Believe me, said Kip silently, you have no competition in this school, Mike Robinson.

"Who are you with, Mike?" she said, unable to stand the suspense.

"Nobody. I didn't know anybody to ask."

Perfect answer. Kip smiled at him, sending messages through her eyes, but whether or not he could interpret them she didn't know.

A pair on the clean-up crew approached her. "Can we start taking down the shed?" they asked.

"Sure, go ahead. It's a prefab workshop that the principal loaned me out of his backyard. It's in six parts. Stack them in his pickup truck, which is parked outside right next to the kitchen door."

"Gotcha."

Roddy said admiringly, "You always have everything lined up, don't you, Kip?"

"Yes," she said, and prayed that he would forgive her for lining something else up, too. "Roddy, do you feel like working with me? I have to stay until clean-up is finished."

Pure fib. She had arranged everything under another kid's supervision because she had not expected to be at the dance. Roddy, of all people, should see through this fib. But he nodded eagerly, ready to help. She winced. "You could start with the fountain," she said. "It's hollow underneath and you wind up the hose and — "

"I know how it works. No problem." Roddy trotted off.

Mike was grinning widely. She didn't know if he understood exactly what was going on or if he just liked to grin. But years of being in charge of things had taught her that as a rule nobody ever knows what is going on and you have to guide them every little step of the way. So she guided Mike the first step of the way. "I'm giving a party myself next week, Mike," she said, which was another fib. They were coming to her as easily as rain tonight. "I'd love to have you come. You can meet some of my friends."

I can ask Con and Anne, she thought. Let them know we're all friends no matter what. And Beth Rose and Gary. Might as well shore up that relationship while I'm at it. Never let it be said that Kip lets a person down. And why not toss in Emily and that cute boy she brought. She has possibilities and I never even noticed.

Mike said, "Great. I'd love to."

She left it at that. No point in overdoing it.

They looked at each other before Kip went to work with the crew. It was a long thoughtful look, but Kip found you can't really figure out anything from a glance. You have to have words to go with it. But one thing for sure. He was interested. He was thinking about her.

"I'll help dismantle the shed," he offered.

"Thank you."

He walked away while she planned the party menu. If her parents were doing something next weekend, they would have to do it somewhere else. And preferably take her four brothers with them.

But they would. Her parents were terrific. Her mother would love the whole idea of the party and hurl herself into the planning of it. She would make only one request. Let me get a good peek at this Mike first, she'd say, and then we'll leave you to your own devices.

My own devices are pretty sneaky, Kip thought, grinning as widely as Mike had. Definitely a hunter with a bright flash. And look what showed up in the light!

At the moment she had the least control, Anne felt the most controlled. Do you suppose someday I will be grateful to Con for walking out the door, she thought, for leaving me all alone for an hour to think?

What pleasure lay in the warm clasp of Con's hand, in the tapping of the snare drums, in the rustling of the dresses of a hundred dancers pressed together.

There were terrible, inevitable scenes ahead, and she felt ready for them. There is nothing on earth I want more, thought Anne, than my mother's good opinion and my mother's good advice. I don't know if that's good or bad, if it's the result of being smothered or the result of being loved. But it's true.

She knew that the scenes would pass. Her mother would be deeply shocked because Anne had betrayed her. But her mother loved her. And in the morning, her mother would be there.

And Con?

She did not have answers about Con because they hadn't asked the questions yet. She did not know if he was strong enough to stay. She did not know if *she* was strong enough, when each and every solution ahead was frightening. Anne cherished every step, every breath, because for her it might really be the last dance: the end of carefree student years, the end of herself and Con.

She looked into Con's eyes, but they were closed. What thoughts Con was lost in she would never know, and maybe never understand.

But tonight he was here, and tonight he would stand with her, and she would cling to that.

The last dance.

Beth Rose stood alone.

Gary had joined the cleanup crew and was working with a vengeance. Did he work so hard because he liked work? Or because it spared him another dance with her?

She twined the lace in her long fingers.

Thank you, Aunt Madge. Your dress got me in the door. It gave me the first night I've ever had of the kind girls dream about. Maybe Gary is just like Virgil Hopkinson. Handsome, but boring. I'd still like a chance to find out. I threw his penny in the fountain. Perhaps wishes really do come true.

But now the fountain was gone.

Roddy was fishing around getting up all the change, putting it in a thick, gold-yellow envelope, marking it with a Magic Marker. How like Kip to have remembered everything, including the charity to which the coins went, the envelope in which it would be delivered, the marker with which it would be addressed. Beth Rose was filled with admiration for Kip.

Gary lifted one section of the shed and set it

on top of a big dolly that would wheel it all out.

My first true love, thought Beth, but she was able to laugh at herself. All sixty minutes of it. Or was it a hundred and twenty minutes? Or do I get to count the entire Saturday night?

He was my knight in shining armor. My coach in four. My magic Cinderella pumpkin.

They were taking away the unsmashed pumpkins now. Most of them were enormous, a foot across, with big curved stem handles. But one was very small. She picked it up. Not a long-lasting souvenir, she thought. But oh so Cinderella!

Christopher slept.

Molly waited at intersections for utility trucks, fire trucks, police cars, ambulances, all of whom must be out there rescuing somebody from something. Don't stop for me, no, of course not, she thought savagely. When has anybody ever stopped for me?

She parked closer to the high school front door than before. An awful lot of people had already left. Good. Kip's dance had failed. Leaving Christopher snoring in the car, Molly entered the building again. Stopping to check her hair and makeup in the girls' room, she went on into the cafeteria with her chin high and her eyes bright.

Instantly she knew it was the last dance.

The cafeteria no longer even looked like the scene of a dance, but more like some impromptu thing among a lot of meaningless props. The lights were too strong, the decorations looked feeble, the food was gone. But her jealousy remained high, because the couples who were there were dancing slow and intensely, locked in each other's arms and hearts. Coldly, Molly checked the room for the only two boys she knew of who were possibilities.

And there he was. Handsome as ever, working with the clean-up crew. Perfect, she thought. He's already abandoned Beth Rose. Easy target.

She threaded her way through the dancers to Gary, calling out his name, putting on her best smile and her flirtiest manner. It never failed her, and it didn't this time, either: Gary looked up instantly, and smiled into her eyes. Keeping her eyes fixed on his, Molly moved toward him, tossing her head, flouncing her skirt — the little things that attracted attention. It worked. His smile stayed on her, and warmed her heart.

Her foot was enveloped by slimy disgusting wetness that seemed to crawl right up her ankle. Molly screamed, jerked back, and stared in horror at the orange stuff all around her.

Gary's sweet smile turned into a wide grin. "Pumpkin," he said. "Here. Have a paper towel. Mop up."

Molly gritted her teeth. Make the best of it, she ordered herself. Pretending to be unsteady as she cleaned her shoe off, she clung to his arm. Gary even put his other hand out to steady her when she began hopping a little.

"Why didn't you warn me, you terrible boy, you?" she said teasingly.

"Terrible boys are like that," he said. "Locked into lousy manners."

227

She laughed. "You have lovely manners, Gary. Always did."

"Thank you."

"Gary?"

"Mmmm?"

He was using a snow shovel to clean up the pumpkin. Molly felt confused, but didn't dwell on it. So he was the nonverbal type. Who cared? Whatever Gary lacked in speech he made up for in body. "It's the last dance, Gary." Her hand lay gently on his sleeve. Somehow, in spite of the task he had undertaken, he was completely clean, looked as if his tuxedo and pants had just been pressed, and his hair just brushed. She liked that in a boy.

"Really?" he said.

"Really."

He gave her that wonderful smile. The one every girl at Westerly flipped over. The one even their *mothers* flipped over. He took her hand in his, smiled right into her eyes, wrapped her fingers around the snow shovel, and said, "Thanks for telling me. I'd better find Beth."

The temptation to kick him harder than she had ever kicked anything in her life was so great that Molly's knuckles turned white holding the shovel. She came very very close to lifting a shovelful of pumpkin and hurling it all over his perfect suit, so she could ruin his perfect night.

She stopped herself.

There was always Roddy. Always. He was a sap, but an easy one. Her batting average was too good to miss with him as well. She whirled, marched over to the fountain he was tinkering with, knelt down beside him, and said without preliminaries, "I'm sorry, Roddy."

He stared at her.

"I've been so bad to you. All night I've watched you and I've felt so awful. You were with Kip and I was with Christopher and oh, Roddy, how I missed being with you!" She let herself cry, opening her eyes wide so the tears would spill over. Letting herself go limp, she sagged next to him and whispered, "I'm so sorry."

"It's okay, Molly," he said hastily, undone by the tears.

"Roddy, forgive me?" She put her hand on his cheek and now it was Roddy's turn to go limp. "Sure," he said. Clumsily he tried to kiss her, but the fountain was in the way and they were crouching. Molly drew him to his feet. "Last dance, Roddy," she murmured. "Please dance it with me."

He looked uncertain. "I kind of came with Kip."

"Of course you did. And I admire your loyalty. But Kip is over there straightening things. And you and I — oh, Roddy, what better way to get back together again than a long slow dance?"

She linked her fingers behind his neck, looking soulfully up at him, and then drew one thumb teasingly along his hairline. Half pouting, half kissing, she said, "Please?"

Roddy fell. As if all her meanness to him had never been, he could not ignore the delight of having Molly beg for his, Roddy's, presence. He gave a silly little laugh, and they snuggled up against each other. Resting her head against his chest, Molly checked out the other couples in the room. Nobody was dancing any closer. He would do, poor sap Roddy, till something better came along.

Gary said, "If you can dance holding a pumpkin, may I have this dance?"

He was laughing. Beth had never heard him laugh out loud before. "It's my coach in four," she told him. "Any moment now my fairy godmother will wave her wand and send me home in style."

He shook his head. "All I have to offer is a six-year-old Chrysler."

"Magic is in the eye of the beholder," she said. "I'll take it."

They danced. Gary held the hand that held the pumpkin, which was awkward, but it made them laugh, and the rest of the dancers looked over at them and laughed with them.

He said, "The photographer told me the pictures would be ready in about two weeks."

She had forgotten the pictures.

"When they come," Gary said, "let's have supper at my dad's restaurant and look at them."

Oh, penny. You were pretty powerful, she thought. What a wish I made on you!

She waved the tiny pumpkin at him. "I'll make pumpkin pie."

He laughed. "Well, you might be able to make one slice."

"We'll share it," she said.

He nodded and danced on.

I think, Beth Rose said to herself, I think I'm going to let myself fall in love after all. The worst thing that can happen is that nothing will happen. And the best thing that can happen is us.

Together.

The last dance.

Emily, feeling like a queen in her blue jeans, and Matt, king, as he swam in her father's blue jeans, were ready to leave. Emily was limping. Her foot was throbbing because the pain killers had long since worn off. Totally disregarding the doctor's orders, she danced anyhow.

Now it was hitting her.

"Matt, I can't walk another step. I'm sorry. It hurts so bad I'm starting to cry." She did cry, apologizing, weeping, and apologizing again. She was unable to put weight on her foot for another moment.

"The pain hit me so fast!" she said, gasping. "Oh, Matt, I'm going to whimper like a puppy hit by a car."

Somebody brought Emily's coat. Matt helped her into it. Perhaps because she was so tired, the pain covered everything else. She was barely aware of the dance, of Matt, the music, or anything but the cuts in her foot.

Putting one arm around her waist, Matt bent

over, and tucked the other arm behind her knees. Before Emily really knew what was happening, he had picked her up in his arms.

Like a groom carrying his bride over the threshold, Matt swung Emily around, showing off his strength. Emily loved it. The rest of the kids clapped, laughing.

"How are you two getting home?" asked Kip, taking charge, as always.

"Her dad is coming," said Matt.

"Somebody go see if Mr. Edmundson is here," Kip called out. "I don't know how long Matt can hold this pose!"

"Is it up to me?" said Emily, smiling into Matt's face. "I think he should maintain it forever."

Matt grinned. "I might," he said. "I just might."

Epilogue

What matters most to every human being is to be loved, and to love in return. Five girls ended their last dance, thinking only of love.

Emily had had the courage to face her worst fear, and to conquer it, and end a winner, truly suspended in loving arms.

Beth Rose had had the courage to walk alone, and had come one step closer to her own dream of love.

Anne had had the courage to admit her private nightmare, and she was one step deeper in the worst dream of her life — but she was also one step closer to herself, and to the boy she loved.

Molly used people, and had neither love nor courage, but she did not know the difference, and Saturday night had not taught her a thing.

And Kip, who had all the love and courage in the world, but nobody yet to give them to, knew only one thing for sure: The dance was hers. Whatever memories the other dancers had, she, Kip, had given them.

Saturday night faded.

Sunday morning began.

The dance was over.